Coffee Break Reads

by

Linda Barrett
and
Rob Nisbet

First published 2014

ISBN: 978-1-326-06380-1

Copyright © The Authors 2014
The moral rights of the authors have been asserted.

The stories contained within this book are works of fiction. Names and characters are the product of the authors' imaginations and any resemblance to actual persons, living or dead, is entirely coincidental.

All rights reserved.
No part of this publication may be reproduced, stored in a retrieval system or transmitted in any form without the written permission of the authors.

Contents

A Charmed Life	6
A Match Made in Maths	11
Better Than Any Son	15
Captive	19
Friday the Thirteenth	22
Festering Beneath	28
Human Resources	32
Great Aunt May	36
Incident at Balcombe	44
Off the Shelf	51
Jean's Bread Pudding	57
Something's Bothering Bill	66
Just a Very Small Slice of Cake	69
The Children's Car Park	74
Rescue Line	77
The Good Samaritan	84
The Christmas Do	88
Twenty-One Today	95
Turn Around	100
Updating Dora	103

A CHARMED LIFE

by Rob Nisbet

"I'm sorry about this Mrs Rodgers, but the doctor would like one more blood test."

"Now?" Silvia struggled to lift her head awkwardly from the pillow. "Ruddy vampire. Doesn't he know I'm about to have a baby?"

The midwife smiled her sympathy but stood her ground, she would not be put off. Obediently Silvia lay back with a sigh, her left palm upwards while the midwife tapped at her elbow joint coaxing a vein to the surface.

"Just another little scratch Mrs Rodgers. I guess by now your arm must feel like a pin cushion," she said as she inserted the needle. "Odd sort of scabbing..." She studied the other needle marks as she drew out a syringe of deep red liquid. "Doesn't look like dried blood, more like they've rusted over."

Silvia gave a sharp whimper and clutched at her bulging stomach with her free hand.

"Another contraction?" The midwife pressed a ball of cotton wool over Silvia's latest puncture. She placed the syringe in a dish and passed this to a young nurse who scuttled out with it for analysis. "Your husband had better hurry up or he'll miss the birth."

Silvia lay back on the hospital bed and tried to breathe normally. That's when the midwife noticed her wrist.

"Your bangle," she said. "A charm bracelet is it? Do you want to take it off? It looks very tight pressing into your wrist like that."

Silvia held the bracelet out for inspection. "It doesn't come off," she said, "there's no clasp."

"Must be." The midwife took a closer look. "Well I never. How on earth did you get it on in the first place? Did you slip it on when you were younger and your wrist a bit thinner?"

"Something like that," Silvia said. But the truth was even stranger.

The midwife was feeling around the chain. "It's definitely too tight," she said. "Look here, it's caused some sort of inflammation under the skin – a hard bump. We'll sort out baby first, but later we'll get a doctor to look at that wrist – probably have to cut off the bracelet I'm afraid. What metal is it? It's not silver – too dull, is it pewter, something like that?"

Silvia shrugged; she had no idea what metal it was – if indeed it was a real metal at all.

"Matches your earrings I see," said the midwife. She examined the shiny-grey hoops. "That's unusual," she said, "your hoops have no clasp or catch either – they look like a solid circle passing through your ear lobes. How's that done then, eh? Is it like two half circles that slot together?"

Silvia grinned, glad of the distraction. "No. I had my ears pierced when I was ten or eleven, they got quite messy and infected at the time – I couldn't wear my studs 'cos of this discharge. Anyway, this metallic pewter-like stuff was coming out of the hole where my ear was pierced, like a thin strand oozing out of the front and back of each ear. I didn't like to touch them, and in a few days the strands had joined together and thickened into these hoops. They look like earrings, but whatever they are, they're part of me."

The midwife gave Silvia a reproachful look; she clearly didn't believe a word. She tilted the watch that hung over her left breast and, as if on cue, Silvia convulsed with another contraction. "Won't be long now," she said. She pulled absently at her own ear lobes. "I could never stand the thought of having my ears pierced. It's funny isn't it that I can happily poke needles into other people all day but can't abide them near myself." She laughed, "You won't find me getting my belly button skewered."

Silvia felt the contraction ease – that had been the strongest one yet. She sighed. "You won't approve of Stan then, when he gets here. He's got piercings everywhere!"

The midwife glanced at the doorway to the corridor. The nurse should be back with the blood test results any moment – she knew how urgent they were. And the doctors wanted to be called if the iron level of Silvia's blood was still high. She turned back to her patient, turning on her reassuring chat. "These piercings of – Stan's, was that his name? – are they normal or did some metal extrude out of holes he made in himself?" She laughed, not expecting an answer. "Let's have another look at your chain – I read in a magazine that you can tell a lot about a person by their choice of charms on a bracelet."

Silvia held out her wrist for inspection.

"Why, they're just blobs," said the midwife. "Shapeless blobs – not charms at all."

But Silvia knew otherwise: At the time she'd thought it just another stage of puberty when she felt the ring of bumps beneath her skin. She hadn't mentioned it, even to her mum or her friends – it was sort of embarrassing – another symptom of how her body was growing up. In time the bumps had grown through the skin of her wrist, segments of a perfect chain linked together to form a bracelet. Silvia knew that it was a part of her, attached tightly round her wrist. Like her earrings it had a metallic sheen but she'd no idea what they were really composed of, bone perhaps.

The bracelet looked tight but it didn't hurt, so Silvia just accepted it as part of her arm. Just as she accepted the appearance of the charms over the years. There had been that car accident. Silvia wasn't expected to survive, but she pulled through – and had gained a charm in the process. They seemed to form at periods of her life of emotional overload. Her first experience of teenage love, the day her father died, her wedding — they may look like shapeless blobs to the midwife, but Silvia knew that they were charms. Each one forged by her own body and added to the chain like a physical memory.

Several things then happened at once.

Stan appeared flushed but grinning, shown through the door by the young nurse with the blood-test results.

The midwife nodded to Silvia. "I see what you mean," she said gesturing to Stan's pierced eyebrow, nose and the dull metal spike just below his lower lip. Silvia had said he was pierced *everywhere* but speculation of these locations would have to wait. The midwife took one glance at the test results — as before, iron levels and metallic traces in the blood were off the scale. She dispatched the nurse immediately to fetch the doctors — but she doubted they'd arrive before the birth. Silvia, with Stan at her bedside, was wracked by another contraction.

It was a girl. She had bewildered looking blue eyes, a downy film of dark hair and a healthy glow to her still-wrinkled skin. Silvia and Stan brimmed with joy at their new arrival.

The midwife washed her hands. The doctors hadn't turned up yet — luckily it had been a straight forward birth, no complications, and a beautiful new baby.

In the sudden bustle of activity not even Silvia had noticed that the hard swelling at her wrist had erupted into a new charm on her bracelet — another emotional experience made physical. Her metallic blood traces would now drop to normal for a while — as if to confuse the medical staff even further.

All attention, naturally, was switched to the new baby, who began to cry in Silvia's arms.

"She's got a good pair of lungs, that one," said the midwife. "That's a healthy sign."

Silvia cuddled her precious daughter close as her new blue eyes creased with her crying. And a glistening tear slid like quicksilver down her tiny cheek.

First published in My Weekly, 2009

A Match Made in Maths

by Linda Barrett

"Jack, you sit next to Lottie, please. You can help her with her algebra."

Yes! Lottie Sinclair is the most popular girl in school. She's tall with long, blonde hair and totally stunning. And she's good at sport, all sport, and she can dance like no one else I've ever seen. You can never get near her at the school discos. There's always a gang of lads waiting to elbow out her mates to have a dance with her. Every one of them in lower sixth has asked her out. Every one except me, that is. And she's knocked them all back.

Me? I'm not one of the lads. I'm not good at sport or dancing. People say I'm nerdy but I don't think I'm all that bad looking. Well, I'm not revolting anyway. I'm just not one of them. They all think I'm a bit weird. One thing I am though, I am very good at maths.

I get up and make my way over to Lottie. The other lads glare at me. Some of them laugh. The girls nudge each other and giggle. As I pull out the chair to sit down Lottie looks up and smiles. My heart soars and I blush, mutter something incomprehensible, and sit down.

"Right!" says Mr. Frost looking around, "I think everyone who is struggling with their equations is sitting next to a proverbial 'bright spark'. Work in pairs. The problems you have to solve are on the board so get on with it."

He sits at his desk at the front and the entire class looks at the board. Then gradually, pair by pair, everyone starts to work. I feel awkward and I feel my face burning again as I turn to her. But this is my thing and I soon feel confident.

Within five minutes, and as we knew he would, old Frosty is nodding. Nobody messes about though. No one ever messes about in Frosty's class.

The forty minutes flies by. I haven't ventured any conversation outside of the algebra that we're doing. Then the bell goes.

She turns and smiles at me. "Will you sit next to me in every maths lesson?" she asks.

I feel like jumping up and punching the air. "Sure," I say simply and I quietly get up, gather my things together and leave with the rest of the class.

"Hey, Weirdo!" the voice comes from behind and I know who it is and that it's aimed at me. I ignore it. "Oi! Morris! I'm talking to you."

This time I turn around to face my nemesis. His name is Mick Wallace, commonly known as 'Bruiser' for obvious reasons. As the name suggests he's one of the biggest bullies in the school and, unfortunately, he's in my class. Since my first day at senior school he has always taken particular pleasure in making my life miserable. But today I'm on cloud nine and he can't ruin it.

The instant I turn he's in my face and a meaty hand grabs the front of my shirt and pushes me into the wall.

"I suppose you think it's your birthday, Loser," his face is now only inches away from mine. I don't answer.

He pushes me harder into the wall. "Don't get any ideas, Morris. She don't like losers." He gives me a final push against the wall, smirks and saunters off. I straighten my clothes, brush myself down and strangely feel a tingle of satisfaction. Bruiser is jealous.

And he isn't the only one. In the weeks that follow one or two smart alecs try to usurp me from my place next to 'the goddess' but to my surprise, and everyone else's, the lovely Lottie always plumps for me.

Her maths improved under my guidance and my confidence soared under hers. The spring term of 1977 flew by and on Valentine's Day of that year, as I picked up my books, from the desk, after a maths lesson, I found a card. I opened it up and it read: *I don't think you're weird. I think you're clever and really cool. Be in the coffee bar on Deansgate at 6:30 to find out who this card is from.*

It's Valentine's Day again and I take my eyes off the TV to look at the woman who has been my life and soul mate for the last thirty years. In my eyes she is still as beautiful as ever. Ben is sitting at the dining table doing his homework.

"Can you help me with my sums please, Grandma Lottie," he asks.

She gets up and goes over to him. She looks over his shoulder at what he's doing. "Your granddad will help you with that. He's always been good at sums." Lottie gives me a knowing look and she goes into the kitchen. I get up and go over to help Ben. Lottie comes back into the room and out of the corner of my eye I see her push something behind the cushion of the armchair I've just vacated. I know what it is and without looking I know what it says.

The coffee shop on Deansgate has long gone. A nice, cosy bistro took its place. After we've dropped Ben off home I'll go to the golf club and Lottie will go shopping. Then we'll meet there at 6:30 tonight just like we do every year.

First published in That's Life Fast Fiction, 2012

Better Than Any Son

by Rob Nisbet

It was six o'clock in the morning, dark and still bitterly cold. The sun wouldn't rise over the distant horizon for another couple of hours and the clear black sky glittered with the light from those other stars, so phenomenally distant that they might as well be made of ice.

Patience gazed up at the sky. Its vast emptiness seemed to suck the heat out of her but it held her transfixed. This was one of the wonders of Botswana. She'd travelled far from the bustle of Gaberone; there was no light pollution here, just the misty stripe of the Milky Way slicing through the heavens above the Kalahari.

Patience shivered and turned back to her tent. It was cold now but the temperature here swung between two extremes and she needed to make a move if she was to reach her goal before the midday heat made any progress unbearable.

Though she was alone, she could hear her father's voice, ever cautious, ever protective. "Always check under the flaps and the ground sheet. You never know what may have crept there overnight." Patience smiled at the memory. "Yes, Dad," she said to the empty desert as she carefully checked for snakes and scorpions that could crawl into the smallest of spaces.

The tent was clear. She rolled it into her rucksack and took a deep gulp of cold water from one of several reassuringly heavy flasks. She picked up the only non-essential item she had with her: a terracotta jar. She reflected that, in a country where even the currency was named after water, this jar contained something far more precious to her than the vital flasks of liquid she carried. She tucked the jar into the crook of her left arm as if cradling a baby and set off northwards.

To her right the sky had started to brighten, drawing long shadows out from the base of each stunted thorn tree that dotted the landscape. She nodded to the ice-stars overhead – melted from view by the rising sun. She'd see them again in the evening, creeping over that same eastern horizon when the sun and its blistering heat faded from the sky.

The first time Patience had made this journey she had been almost seven. She was an only child and had accompanied her father, in the absence of a son, on this trail of family tradition. That's when she'd first learnt the safety rules of surviving away from the town.

In the evening she would collect armfuls of the baked-dry sticks needed for the cooking fire. She always collected more than the boys – they just weren't used to having to fend for themselves – and more than once her keen eyes had prevented one of the sons from grabbing hold of a snake hiding in the dead branches.

"Better than any son." That's what her father had said to the other men, in the evenings, as they sat around the glowing fire. Its heat warmed them as the cold night swept like a tide over the bleak landscape, and the flames kept back any creatures that might otherwise have crept too close. Of course the other men had disagreed, especially those with sons of their own. Patience had felt so proud, both in herself and in her father. He had gone against all prejudice and tradition to bring his daughter along, and then to speak-out in her favour in front of his own elders… But then, this whole tradition was itself a process of change; the old were replaced by the young. Old ideas, unless they still held some worth or relevance died and were forgotten. New concepts came into being with fresh generations – only certain values remained eternal.

Patience smiled as she thought of her father's pedantic, caution. He seemed slow in today's ever quickening world. But it had served him well. It was hard now to imagine that in his day he had been the rebel pushing against the prejudices of his elders – pushing their limits, getting his seven-year-old daughter accepted even in this most male of ceremonies. It was a demonstration of his love for his family – and that was eternal, like the stars.

The seven-year-old Patience had watched from the background as the ceremony unfolded. Her grandfather's ashes had been poured onto the Kalahari with great solemnity and chanting, ringed by his sons and grandsons – and one granddaughter.

Now it was her father's turn. Patience clutched the terracotta jar to herself and continued to walk, amazed that in this shifting almost featureless environment she could remember the way. Her sandals flicked up the red dusty earth, only a few more miles, only a few more hours to go.

Finally Patience reached the correct spot. Why this particular area had been selected Patience didn't know, and it was too late now to ask her father. Another tradition, no doubt based on the male ego and having to trek deep into the wilderness. But it was what her father would have wanted, and that was all the justification Patience needed.

She had made good progress; there were still a couple of hours till midday. She took a long drink from one of her flasks thankfully shrugging off the backpack and tent that she would need again on her way home.

With great care, Patience unstoppered the terracotta jar. She tried to be serious but memories of her father always made her smile. She missed him of course, but a life is to be celebrated! How else could she move on, push back at the old traditions. What would her own grandfather have thought of her – a daughter, alone in this most male of places, and with so important a mission?

The sun poured down on the desert, bleaching away the old traditions, glowing over the lone figure of Patience who twirled with the jar, dancing its contents into the Kalahari, a smile on her lips and a tear in her eye.

First published in My Weekly, 2010

Captive

by Linda Barrett

Despite the midsummer heat the supermarket car park was as busy as ever. Drivers, queuing for a space, were becoming irritable as they watched for people loading up, hoping that they were getting ready to move out. Mothers in light cotton dresses were coaxing complaining children inside. Husbands were helping their wives to carry their purchases to their cars. Some were carrying bags and others were pushing trolleys. It was pretty much a normal Saturday afternoon.

The silver Vectra stood innocuously in one corner. People came, did their shopping and went on their way. No one noticed it. Why should they? They had no reason to suspect how long the car had been there or what was taking place inside it.

The temperature kept rising as the sun beat down relentlessly. How much longer? He banged the windscreen yet again. If anyone heard or saw him they didn't acknowledge the fact. He laid his head on the hot, plastic dashboard. Would they care when they found him? Would they be racked with guilt?

His friends would miss him. If nothing else he was a good worker. Then there were his brothers. Maybe they would find him. No, they'd be hard at it at this time of day.

He watched the activity from the confines of his scorching, suffocating prison. A young mother was dragging a screaming child, of about three, to a car a couple of rows away. She looked hot and harassed as she carried two, overflowing carrier bags in one hand and held the child firmly by his arm with the other.

He jumped as he heard a door slam in the car parked next to the Vectra. He darted to the side window. A middle-aged man had just slammed the boot door down and was pushing his empty trolley between the two cars to take it back to the trolley park. He threw himself at the window but the man didn't see.

Pure determination seized him. He wouldn't give up just like that!

Frantically, and for the umpteenth time, he meticulously examined every millimetre of the car, every window, every door, the roof, but there was no means of escape. It was shut tight. The sun continued to beat down and in despair he finally fell, exhausted, onto the back seat. All he could do was wait for the end.

There was no air inside now and the heat was unbearable. He started to lose consciousness. He didn't care anymore. He just wanted it all to be over.

He sank deeper and deeper into oblivion. Pictures of a beautiful garden floated into his mind. Was it only a matter of hours ago that he was there? The exquisite flowers, the vibrant colours. He could actually smell the heady scent of the roses.

What seemed like a hundred other summer days flitted through his mind, the warm sunshine, the flora, the smell of newly cut grass. He tried to open his eyes. It couldn't be all over. Not yet! What if he tried just one more time to attract someone's attention or find a way out? No, he was clutching at straws. He didn't even have the energy left to try. Perhaps someone would come looking for him. Again, he thought of his brothers. They probably hadn't even realised he was missing yet. He sank further into the void.

After what seemed an eternity a back passenger door opened but he was too weak to move. A man and woman were arguing. The man was complaining to her.

"Come on. We were only supposed to be going to the supermarket not all over town."

"Well, if you'd let me drive the car I'd go on my own."

Her companion sighed heavily. "Okay, let's get them in and go home."

The woman began hurriedly tossing bulging carrier bags onto the back seat. Along with the fresh air came an inner strength. He came to and instantly registered the situation.

He moved quickly as one of the bags came within a hair's breadth of squashing him. Wasting no time he headed for the open space and life. She gave a little squeal as he brushed past her and she shuddered.

He took to the air and, buzzing merrily, he made his way back to his hive.

First published in The Weekly News, 2010

Friday the Thirteenth

by Rob Nisbet

"Jill, what's wrong? Why are you whispering?" Carla's voice sounded frantic. "Something's the matter isn't it? I knew it – I just knew there'd be a disaster, today of all days."

Jill winced and held the mobile away from her ear. "Carla, don't shout... I don't want to be noticed." She held the phone close to her lips. "That's why I'm whispering."

Carla's voice dropped a few decibels. "You sound muffled. Jill, what's going on?"

"I'm hiding – under the duvet."

"So you really *are* spending the day in bed." Carla was impressed. "Hang on – did you say *hiding*?"

Jill slid her head from under the bedding and risked a cautious glance toward the bright window. Figures moved beyond the net curtain, but she sighed with relief. There was no sign of them peering through into her bedroom, at least not yet.

"I'm an idiot," said Jill, a little louder. "I didn't pull the curtains and I left the main window open last night. Then when the phone rang, I was sure they'd hear it and be looking in at me."

"Who's *they*?"

"The men outside the window."

"But..." Carla paused, as if she might have misunderstood. "Jill, you live on the first floor!"

Jill pulled herself up onto the pillows. "I complained to the landlord about the cracks in the concrete stairs, you know – leading up to the front door."

"Quite right," said Carla with approval. "Cracks are very unlucky."

"I know. I didn't think he'd take me seriously – just because I'm superstitious, but I pointed out that a cracked step could be dangerous. I had to practically foxtrot up and down the stairs to avoid stepping on them. Anyway, the landlord actually listened for once. More than listened; he has a team of workmen out there now, repairing the steps. And while they're at it they're smoothing over the cracks in the walls too. Trouble is – that means scaffolding and workmen right outside my window."

"I see..." said Carla. "You poor thing; there you are, safely staying in bed all day – and this happens. It's fate. Nothing will go right today, you mark my words."

"I know. I'm in my skimpy teddy-bear jim-jams too. It couldn't *be* more embarrassing." Jill pulled the duvet up to her chin. "There's three men, right outside, fastening together loads of poles and planking." She watched as a burly young man with a dark beard, tightened the joint where two poles met. Despite the cloudy day he wore a thin burgundy t-shirt and Jill watched his muscles flex as he worked the wrench. It was bright outside, she could see him clearly enough. That made her worry even more, could he see as clearly into her bedroom?

"Carla." Jill's voice had dropped again. "It might be my imagination, but one of the men... His eyes keep flicking in this direction."

There was a shout from outside and the man turned, looking down. He reached out and hauled up a wooden stepladder. Jill groaned.

"What's happening?" Carla's voice was anxious.

"Ladders!" said Jill. "That settles it. I'm trapped. There's no way I can venture out now, not with ladders above the entrance."

Carla agreed. "Walking under ladders is always unlucky. To knowingly walk under one today – well that's just asking for trouble."

"What should I do?" Jill asked. "I'm sure if I get out of bed, they'll see the movement. I'd die of embarrassment."

"You could tell them the truth," Carla suggested.

"They'd think I'm crazy." She affected a sing-song chatty voice. "Hello boys, I know it's the middle of the day but I'm paranoid about it being Friday the thirteenth, so I'm staying in bed."

"Sounds reasonable to me."

"You're not the one with three blokes about to ogle you through the window."

"Are you sure you're not asleep?" asked Carla, a tinge of mischief in her voice. "This could be some dream fantasy."

"Carla!" Jill realised she'd spoken too loudly and shot a glance at the window. "Hey, good news. Two of them have gone up the ladder to the next floor. That just leaves the one with the beard, tightening joints."

"A beard?" Jill could hear Carla flicking through the pages of a book. "Here it is: pogonophobia – a fear of beards. You'd better be careful."

"Fear of beards?" Jill was quietly scornful. "I've never heard of it."

"It's here in my book of superstitions and phobias – so there must be something to it. Most fears have a rational explanation, you know. Fear of heights, fear of spiders, that sort of thing – It's your body's subconscious way of avoiding danger. Self preservation, it's instinctive."

"Yeah, that makes sense – but *beards?*"

"Doesn't matter how obscure or irrational a fear is, there'll be a reason for it. Let's see, beards... They're a sure sign of laziness in a man – and it means he's got something to hide."

"Something to hide?" Jill found herself watching the tight burgundy t-shirt. "Not from what I can see."

"Jill! You're incorrigible! Don't forget your window's open – he might hear you."

"Hey Carla, he's moved along the scaffolding, towards the kitchen. Now's my chance."

"You going to get dressed, quickly?"

"No way! I'm not taking my clothes off, and I daren't go near the window; he could turn back at any moment. And with my luck so far today, that's *exactly* what would happen."

Jill flicked back the duvet and tip-toed towards the door, easing the lace-edging of her shorts as far down her legs as seemed prudent.

"Jill – what's happening? Don't go silent on me now."

"It's OK; I'm nearly at the door. I've got a thick towelling robe in the bathroom. Damn."

"What now?"

"I just remembered – last night I put my robe in the washing bin – and that's in the kitchen."

"With your fantasy builder just outside the window. Any net curtains?"

"Nothing at all."

"It's Friday the thirteenth all right; how much more can go wrong?"

Jill peered cautiously around the kitchen door. She could clearly see the bearded man busy outside the window, and there, balanced on the window ledge above the washing machine, was the laundry basket. Her pink towelling robe rested on the top, tantalizingly just out of reach. "I've got an idea," she whispered into the phone.

She withdrew to the hallway and bathroom, returning with a long furled red umbrella and her round make-up mirror on a stand, relaying her movements all the time to Carla. "I'm sliding the mirror as far as I can reach along the kitchen tiles."

"What for? So you can spy on your hunky builder?"

"No!" Jill strained around the kitchen door waving the umbrella, her phone jammed between her cocked ear and shoulder. "I can use the mirror to see what I'm doing. If I stand on one leg and reach forward I can hook the laundry basket and pull it towards me."

"I see. Well, considering what day it is – good luck."

Jill held the point of the umbrella, waving the hooked end around the door. The reversed image in the mirror confused her sense of direction and she waved the handle wildly over the packets and cartons on the work surface. She raised one leg higher behind her to keep her balance as she swung the umbrella again.

"Touch wood," said Carla.

Instinctively Jill reached out to the wooden door frame, losing her concentration, and her balance. She toppled forward. The umbrella handle came down heavily on the basket rim, pressing the button that opened it automatically. The bright red canvas sprung open blocking Jill's view as she fell. She shrieked as she hit the floor, and the umbrella's handle smashed into the mirror.

A broken mirror! Seven years' of bad luck lay splintered around her. An umbrella - open indoors! And on the work surface the salt carton had toppled, spilling a stream of misfortune onto the tiles.

"Hey, you OK?"

It wasn't Carla's voice; the phone was lying somewhere on the floor. Jill turned, looking up. Filling the doorway of her little kitchen was the bearded builder.

"Careful of the glass," he said, stepping forward and offering his hand.

Jill was conscious of her bare feet, then suddenly of her bare legs, arms and plunging lacy neckline! Her hands wavered to cover her body, then held onto the man's arm as he helped her up.

"I heard you cry out," he said. "And your window was open. I noticed it earlier – when you were in bed."

"You saw me in bed!" Jill felt her face burn with embarrassment.

"Couldn't help it." The man's beard broke with a grin. "I sent the other blokes up to the next floor; they wouldn't have been so – subtle."

Jill saw his dark eyes taking-in the bizarre scene. His heavy boots crunched on the broken fragments as he reached for the bath robe.

"This what you wanted?"

Jill nodded dumbly and the man turned towards the sink. "I think," he said, "you need a cup of builders' tea." Then he stooped, sweeping up her mobile in his big hands and passing it to her.

Carla was still gabbling away at the other end, demanding to know what was happening.

"Calm down," said Jill. "I'm OK, I fell, that's all."

"I heard glass breaking, and a man's voice," said Carla with suspicion. "Jill, what's going on?"

"Tell you what," Jill smirked. "Perhaps I was wrong about Friday the thirteenth."

"Oh yes..." Carla's tone was guarded.

Jill's voice dropped, but there was a sparkle in her whisper. "This morning I was so superstitious that I wouldn't even get out of bed. Well, turns out I'm not as paranoid as I thought."

"What do you mean?"

"Mirrors," said Jill. "Umbrellas, salt, cracks, ladders and Friday the thirteenth – seems they're not unlucky after all."

On the other end of the phone Carla gasped in horror.

"And as for pogonophobia – well, I've discovered I don't have a fear of beards either!"

First published in My Weekly, 2012

Festering Beneath

by Linda Barrett

Marie sighed as she picked up the overflowing ashtray yet again. As she was emptying it she looked up at the yellowed walls and the brown stained curtains. She glared at her husband, Jim, who was, as usual, slumped snoring in his armchair. Well, at least he wasn't having a go at her.

Distracted she accidentally dropped the ashtray into the bin. It landed with a clatter.

Jim started, "What the hell are you doing?" he barked.

Marie flinched, "I'm just emptying your ashtray. You should give up, you know. Dr Hamilton warned you what could happen if you don't."

"Put kettle on and stop nagging." He lit another cigarette.

She scurried through to the kitchen, made the tea and carried it through to the living room. He took the mug from her and grunted.

"That boil on my back's really playing up now," he grumbled. "Put another plaster on for me."

Dutifully, she went back into the kitchen to get one from the drawer. She took it through. Jim already had his jumper pulled up over his head and Marie pulled the old one off and pressed the new one firmly into place between his shoulder blades.

"Does it look bad? It bloomin' hurts, I can tell you that," he whined.

"The plasters are drawing it out now, that's all."

Marie picked up her tea and sat down on the sofa to watch the programme, which Jim, of course, had chosen. No sooner had she settled down than he grabbed the remote control and started flicking through the channels.

"They're looking for an assistant at the newsagent's on the road," she ventured tentatively.

"So?"

"Well, a little job like that would give us a bit of extra money and I'm desperate to get out of the house. These four walls are really closing in on me."

Jim leaned forward. His voice was barely audible.

"Are you saying I can't keep you? Is that what you're saying?"

"No, of course not but what if something happened to you?"

"Then you'd have my pension, wouldn't you?"

Marie knew when it was wise to drop a subject so she turned her attention back to the television.

Jim worked overtime on Saturday mornings. He usually got home around one o'clock but today he was early.

"I feel a bit off-colour," he complained. "I haven't felt well all morning. I keep getting pains in my chest."

"Go and sit down," said Marie "and I'll make you a cup of tea."

"You do look a bit peaky," she said as she handed him the mug.

"I feel it. My back's really sore as well. Have a look at it."

Marie lifted up his shirt. "Yes, it does look inflamed. I'll put a new plaster on it," and she went and got one from the kitchen drawer.

Jim eventually laid the empty mug on the coffee table, stubbed out his cigarette and went up to bed. Marie settled down with her cup of tea and some chocolate biscuits to watch one of her favourite films on DVD. It was lovely to be able to watch a film on a Saturday afternoon instead of having the sport blaring out.

He didn't come down for his tea and Marie decided to let him lie. It was about 9:30 before she decided to go upstairs and check on him.

She knew as soon as she saw him that he was dead. He was lying on his back, his eyes wide open, staring but unseeing, at the ceiling.

She phoned the emergency doctor, who turned out to be their GP, Dr. Hamilton. She then rang her sister, Sue. Both were there within half an hour.

"He's suffered a massive heart attack," the doctor said as he sat down next to her on the sofa and took her hand. "I'll phone someone to come and take him away, shall I?"

"Will there have to be a post mortem?" Marie asked. "I don't like to think of him being cut up."

"No. No need for that," the doctor assured her. "I only saw him last week and I warned him then what his heavy smoking could lead to, especially with his high blood pressure. No, the cause is clear enough."

Marie opened her front door, picked up the pile of mail lying behind it and went through to the kitchen. Her sister, Sue, had insisted that she went to stay with her until after the funeral. Well the funeral was over and all the necessary business that goes with a death had been completed. As she'd said to Sue, this morning, she had to get on with her life now.

She opened the letter from Jim's firm's solicitor with trembling hands. Inside was a cheque for £203,207. His pension scheme paid out a handsome lump sum to the next of kin in the event of him not reaching pensionable age.

Next she opened the envelope from her local college. She'd been accepted on the computer course she'd applied for and noted with some trepidation that it started in only two weeks.

Lastly, she opened the drawer in the kitchen table and took out the high strength nicotine patches that she had stored there for the last month. She read the warning on the packet - *It is extremely dangerous to smoke whilst using these patches.*

She opened the pedal bin and threw them inside. Very fortunate that boil appearing when it did. She'd removed the patch from Jim's back before the doctor arrived. Despite his constant moaning about the discomfort it had hardly left a mark on him. Drama Queen! she thought as she closed the lid.

How did the saying go? Ah yes, *Today is the first day of the rest of your life.* Well she was certainly going to make the most of the rest of her life - thanks to Jim.

First published in That's Life Fast Fiction, 2009

Human Resources

by Rob Nisbet

"Well," said Pauline, with an indignant pursing of her magenta lips, "who'd have thought it? When I got out of bed this morning, I never suspected that the whole population of London would have been kidnapped by aliens by lunchtime."

"What do you think will happen to us?" asked a woman at Pauline's side. "I was preparing some soup – then, zap! Here we are queuing in the human resource assessment area."

"Soup!" The alien tentacled past carrying a steaming stripy bowl. It scooped at the soup with a spoon-shaped appendage, while keeping the queue in order. The humans were ushered towards a series of desks.

Pauline, her companion and a gentleman in a suit and tie were waved forward to the first desk. Another alien sat behind it, a bowl of fragrant soup resting among its papers.

"This is an intelligence test," said the alien, scooping at the soup as it spoke. "London was selected because it had the most suitable demographic proportions for our needs."

"Oh yeah, and just what are your needs?" demanded Pauline. "I'm missing daytime telly!"

The alien slurped at its soup. "Our needs are various," it said. "Hence the tests." It passed, what looked to Pauline like an empty picture frame, to each of the humans at the desk, then pointed its spoon-shaped appendage to a pile of irregular blocks.

"The task is to place the blocks in the frame in the most space-saving and efficient manner, and as quickly as possible."

The man in the tie immediately began to fit the blocks into the frame, selecting each one carefully and fitting it into the spaces, leaving no gaps. Pauline, had been so busy complaining that she hadn't followed the instructions. She watched her other companion as she rejected an oddly-shaped block and tried another in her frame. "You're doing it all wrong," said Pauline with a magenta smirk. "Try the blue one."

"Finished," said the man with the tie.

"Stop," commanded the alien.

"Hey, not fair," Pauline protested. "I ain't started."

The alien pointed its spoon at the man. "*You* have passed this first test." A ripple appeared in the air. "Step through," said the alien. "It is a worm-holed inter-dimensional matter transmogrifying doorway."

"But where does it go?" asked the man, not unreasonably.

"It links to our orbiting soup moons. Humans are required to help in the running of the soup factories. You have proven your ability and will be given a managerial post to ensure the smooth efficiency of soup production. Well done."

The man stepped into the ripple and the alien pressed a button on its desk. The button had alien script around it which translated as 'Soup Managers'. The man and the ripple disappeared.

"Next!" said the alien.

Pauline, her companion and several others were marched off to the next desk.

"It was a stupid test anyway," she wagged a finger at her companion. "It was a nerd test, that's what it was. A way to get rid of them! Someone ought to have done it years ago!" They found themselves standing with a different man, facing the next test. "Don't think much of him," Pauline commented to the woman. "He's filthy, like he's just come off a building site. And what's that smell?"

33

"Soup," said the alien. "The next test is for you to identify the ingredients in these soups."

They were each given two small bowls of soup and two spoons.

"That one's chicken; that one's vegetable," said the builder.

"That one's too hot," said Pauline. She tasted the next. "An' yuucck! That one's disgusting!"

"This one is chicken," said the other woman. "Creamy, with sweet corn and a little coriander. The second one is root vegetables, chunky enough to add texture and seasoned with rosemary."

"*You* have been selected," said the alien to Pauline's companion. Another ripple appeared in the air. "This wormholed inter-dimensional matter transmogrifying doorway leads to the kitchens of the soup moons, you will become one of our army of cooks and chefs. Pass through, and well done."

A little nervously Pauline's companion stepped into the ripple. The alien pressed a button on its desk which translated as 'Soup Production Staff'. The woman and the ripple vanished.

"Next!" said the alien, and had a quick slurp from its soup bowl.

"Well," said Pauline, as she was herded forward. "I never wanted to cook carrots for no aliens anyway. That's forced labour, that is. I ain't worked in years. If someone don't want to work, that's their right, that's what I say."

At the next desk Pauline was placed with the builder and a scruffy-jeaned youth with stringy hair hanging from within a hooded top. Pauline twisted her magenta mouth in a don't-think-much-of-these-two face to the alien behind the desk.

The alien slurped at a spoonful of soup then placed before them an intricate system of pipes and valves. "Plumbing!" Pauline was scornful. "What sort of test is this?"

"Your task is to control the flow of soup, from the tank at the top, to the tap at the bottom. Begin!"

Pauline and the youth exchanged sneers of derision while the builder began to twist dials and arrange the piping in an appropriate manner.

"Well done," said the alien to the builder. "You have shown a useful aptitude for maintenance work." Another ripple appeared in the air. "Step into the worm-holed inter-dimensional matter transmogrifying doorway. You will be transported to the soup moons to begin your work."

The builder stepped into the ripple as the alien pressed another button. The script above the button translated as 'Soup Maintenance'.

"There is one final test," said the alien, and waved Pauline, the youth and everyone else on to yet another desk.

At the final desk a worm-holed inter-dimensional matter transmogrifying doorway rippled into existence.

"Your final test is to step through the transportation ripple to the soup moons," said a bored looking attendant alien between slurps from its bowl of soup.

"Is that all?" Pauline stepped forward. She beckoned to the scruffy youth and the others to follow her. "Not much of a test – any idiot could do that."

"Exactly," said the bored alien. "Well done."

The alien pressed the button on the desk. Pauline, and most of the population of London, vanished as the ripple faded away. The script above the button translated as 'Soup Ingredients'.

First published in My Weekly, 2013

Great-Aunt May

by Linda Barrett

Clarissa did not shed a tear when she heard that Great-Aunt May had died. Well, why should she? She hadn't seen her in donkey's years.

"I'll bet she left everything to that loser cousin of mine," she remonstrated to her husband, Brad, over breakfast.

"Jane has been looking after her for the last ten years," he pointed out. "You didn't want to know her. You didn't even respond when Jane sent you that text telling you that Aunt May was seriously ill."

"Unlike dear Jane I'm very busy with the boutique. All she had to do was nurse the old girl. And I'll bet she didn't even pay for her keep."

Brad shook his head. He knew when he was wasting his time.

Taking out her mobile Clarissa read again the text from Jane. *Aunt May has died. I'll be in touch about the funeral arrangements.*

"Very short and sweet. And what about the will? We are her only two living relatives. I'll bet she made sure she feathered her nest before the old lady died."

"Then maybe you should have gone to see her when you had the chance."

Clarissa flew at him. "Oh yes, I've got all the time in the world for visiting old ladies, haven't I?"

He gave up. "I'd better get to work," and he grabbed his briefcase and left.

Wanting to find out what was going on, and not wanting to give Jane time to manipulate anything as regarded Aunt May's possessions, Clarissa decided to phone her and arrange to meet up.

Her cousin seemed pleased to hear from her and they arranged to meet, that very afternoon, at the coffee shop on the High Street.

Jane was already sitting with a cup of tea when Clarissa arrived some twenty minutes late. It didn't occur to her to apologise for her lateness. She sat down in the seat opposite and clicked her fingers to get the waitress's attention.

Then finally turning and looking at the other woman she was a little taken aback at the sight of her red, swollen eyes. She dismissed it almost immediately, assuming that it had all been put on for her benefit. She surveyed her cousin. Still as dowdy as ever, she thought. She's probably never seen the inside of a boutique. A few hours in a gym wouldn't do her any harm either.

"So, poor old Aunt May," she said finally.

At this Jane broke down into floods of tears. "I'm so sorry," she managed between sobs, "but I do miss her. The house is so empty without her."

Clarissa suppressed an urge to tell Jane to pull herself together and instead patted her arm awkwardly.

"So what will you do now?" This might be a good time to find out what was happening to Aunt May's estate. "Will you be able to stay on in the house?"

"Oh, yes! That's not a problem. She left the house to me."

Clarissa bristled. "I see. Did she leave everything to you?"

"No, just the house. She talked about leaving the contents to you."

"And what about her bank accounts and such?" Clarissa's eyes shone but she tried to keep her voice steady.

"Oh, Aunt May didn't believe in banks. She kept all her spare cash in a biscuit tin in the airing cupboard."

That was more like it.

"I got a phone call this morning to say that the funeral will be a week on Wednesday at 11 o'clock," Jane continued. "She wanted to be cremated, you know. I'm putting on some refreshments at the house afterwards and the solicitor is going to come at 2:30 to read the will."

"Well, you'll be able to get on with your life once it's all over. Will you get a job now?"

"I'll have to try. I'll have to make a living somehow. Actually, when I leave you I'm going straight to the job centre to make an appointment and see if anything's going."

It suddenly occurred to Clarissa that whatever was in that tin could be in Jane's purse at any time, if it wasn't already.

"Oh, no need to rush into that. Why don't I come back home with you and have a look at the contents?"

"I really need to get myself a job sorted out as soon as possible."

But Clarissa was not going to be put off. "You can do that tomorrow. We haven't seen each other for years."

Jane reluctantly agreed and Clarissa went home with her to view her inheritance. On the whole she was deeply disappointed. Most of the furnishings were old and tattered.

"I always thought Aunt May had a bob or two?" she pointed out as she looked disdainfully around.

"Well, I don't think she was hard up but I don't know exactly what she was worth. She was very private about such things."

"Where's this biscuit tin, then?"

Jane looked aghast at her bluntness but took her upstairs. She opened the airing cupboard door and extracted the tin in which Aunt May had kept her money. She handed it to Clarissa, who opened it eagerly. As she had hoped it was stuffed full of notes and she was pleased to see some fifties in there. She took the tin downstairs and emptied it out onto the kitchen worktop. She began counting. To her delight the biscuit tin contained £12,140. She was about to cram the notes into her handbag when Jane stopped her.

"We can't take anything until after the will is read. I only said that Aunt May told me that she would leave you the contents. I don't know exactly what's in the will."

Clarissa knew that she was right. "Okay, but I'll just make a note of what's here if you don't mind." She took her diary and a pen out of her bag and, without even noticing the hurt expression on Jane's face, she noted down the amount in the tin. Then she replaced the notes and handed it back to her cousin.

On her way home Clarissa felt much brighter. £12,140 was a lot of money considering she'd hardly known the old girl. Some of that furniture and bits and pieces might also fetch something as antiques. She'd get a dealer in there as soon as the will was read.

Brad was horrified when Clarissa told him that she had no intension of going to the funeral but would just attend the reading of the will later.

"You can't do that for heaven's sake."

"Why? I hate funerals and it's not as if we knew her."

"Clarissa, you are going to make a pretty penny out of her death from the sound of it. The least you can do is to pay your respects."

"Well I'm not." Clarissa sounded like a petulant child. "I'll say I have business to attend to which can't be put off."

Though Brad had never met Aunt May he felt compelled, out of common decency, to take the morning off work and attend the funeral himself. He apologised profusely to Jane for his wife's absence and coloured as he explained that she had important business to see to.

Jane said she understood. "Will you come back to the house for a bite to eat?" she asked him.

"I'd love to but unfortunately I have to get back to work myself. No doubt we'll see you soon."

Jane agreed that this was true and Brad returned to work.

That afternoon Clarissa arrived at Jane's home just before the solicitor was due. There were no surprises in the reading and as her cousin said the house had been left to her and its contents to Clarissa. There was no mention of any bank accounts.

The solicitor left and Clarissa went straight to the airing cupboard to get the tin.

"I have to rush off. A woman's work and all that. I've arranged for an antiques dealer to come tomorrow to assess the contents. We'll be here about ten. I trust you'll be home?" And before Jane could answer she was gone.

Clarissa was pleasantly surprised that the dealer thought that quite a few items of Aunt May's would sell as antiques. He offered to buy them from her and to save herself any hassle she readily agreed.

"What about Jane?" asked Brad later that evening. "I know she's got the house but the rate your going she'll have nothing in it. You've already taken all the cash there was."

"Oh, come on! She'll have to get a job. She got a far better deal out of Aunt May's death than I did."

"It takes time to get a job and in the meantime she has no money and no furniture."

"Nonsense! I'm not taking all the furniture, only the bits that are worth something and I'm sure she'll be able to get some sort of benefit." Knowing that he was beat Brad again retreated.

A couple of weeks later Brad decided to call on Jane to see how she was getting on. The house was sparse to say the least. Clarissa had taken all the electrical items of any value along with the antiques.

To his surprise the garden was full of rubbish and Jane looked hot and tired. "I'm going to have to get rid of the house," she explained, "and find something smaller. A little flat maybe. I just can't afford to keep it on."

"I'm really sorry to hear that," said Brad. "Is there no other way?"

"I can't see one. Anyway, I'm going to have to get rid of one or two things of Aunt May's. I've got someone to come and collect them tomorrow but I have to get it all into the front garden. Once it's gone I can put the cottage up for sale."

"Right, well I'll give you a hand," he said, removing his jacket.

"There's only her bed to go. I was wondering how I would manage it."

"Let's take a look then," and he followed Jane upstairs. Luckily the bed was a single and would be easy enough to dismantle.

"It's seen better days, hasn't it? he observed. "This mattress has been patched up a few times." He pressed down on it with his hands as if to test it for comfort.

A smile suddenly started to play on his lips. "No! She couldn't have. It's much too obvious." Jane looked puzzled. Brad grinned at her. "Fetch me a sharp knife."

Still baffled she went to the kitchen and came back with a sharp knife. Brad took it from her and stabbed the neat stitching on the mattress. Carefully, he started to cut. After he had made a six inch gash along the seam line he put his hand inside. His grin widened. He brought his hand out. Clenched in his fist was a wad of bank notes.

Jane shrieked in delight. They both attacked what was left of the seam and tore the mattress open. They couldn't believe what they found inside. Once satisfied that the mattress was empty of notes they put them in a bag and took them downstairs to count. Incredulously the mattress had contained £57,855.

"Clarissa will be pleased," said Jane when they'd finished counting.

"You must be joking. Clarissa will never know," Brad responded.

"It's hers by rights," she reminded him.

"I think Great-Aunt May wanted you to have it," he said gently. "She knew Clarissa well enough to know that she wouldn't want the mattress. She left her what she thought was fair. You were the one who cared for her and about her. The money is yours. All you have to do is decide what to do with it."

Her face lit up and it struck Brad how pretty she was.

"I won't have to sell the cottage," she threw a pile of notes into the air with a whoop. Then she became thoughtful. "Well, the first thing I'm going to do is to try and buy back all Aunt May's antiques. Get the house back to the home it was. What will you tell Clarissa?"

"Oh, I don't plan on telling her anything. She's away on business for a couple of days. By the time she gets back I'll be gone."

"I'm sorry," Jane said.

"Don't be. It's been a long time coming. As for Clarissa, she'll hardly notice I've gone. Hey how about dinner?" he brightened. "We can celebrate your good fortune."

Jane smiled. "My treat," she said."

As they sat in the restaurant both of them knew that their lives were about to take a turn for the better. They ordered champagne to celebrate Jane's good fortune.

"I'd like to propose a toast," said Brad, raising his glass. "To Great Aunt May." They clinked their glasses together and raised them.

"To Great Aunt May," said Jane.

First published in Diamonds and Pearls 2011

Incident at Balcombe

by Rob Nisbet

Danny kept his head down as the train clattered out of London Bridge, pretending to read the evening paper. He'd had just about as much as he could take from Brian at work; the last thing he wanted was to have his supervisor's company on the way home. The train was getting crowded and Danny was conscious of the empty seat next to him. He tried to hold out the newspaper so that Brian might pass by to a less cramped seat. No such luck.

"Danny." Only Brian could make the name sound so derogatory. "Don't hog all the seats."

"Brian." Danny tried to sound surprised. "I didn't know you used this line."

Brian squeezed onto the aisle seat pushing Danny into the woman on his other side. "I've been commuting round here for ten years now!" he said. He made it sound like an achievement – like he'd earned his seat. "Not like you new kids, been working five minutes and take-up all the seats."

Danny groaned to himself and smoothed-out the paper. With any luck Brian would take the hint and he could carry-on reading. Some hope.

"You've been with the firm, how long now?"

"Nearly three months." It seemed to Danny like three years.

"Yes – I've got your end-of-probation assessment to do." Brian patted the laptop case by his feet, then shook his head sadly. "It's touch and go, Danny."

Danny felt the eyes of everyone around him flick in his direction then away – a sure sign that they were all listening.

"Your time-keeping," said Brian, "lunchtime for example."

Danny couldn't believe Brian was discussing this now. "I've never taken more than the allotted hour."

"I know, Danny; don't get all defensive. But there are many others who just grab a snack and then eat it at their desk. You must have noticed – but then you're not there, are you?"

Danny could feel his embarrassment burning through his cheeks. "Can we not do this now?" he asked. "Not in public."

Brian was shocked. "Well, if you don't want to know how to improve..." He actually raised his voice. "You are borderline, Danny – I don't mind telling you. You've got one more day to pull your socks up or I'll see that you're out by the end of the week. I shall type-up your appraisal on the way home tomorrow." He tapped the laptop again. "I don't mind putting in a few extra hours. If only all the staff were like me."

Brian paused, twisting in his seat to give Danny an appraising once-over. Danny just knew that he shouldn't have loosened his tie the instant he'd left the office. Brian had noticed. "That's another thing..." he began. The passengers were treated to a list of Danny's failings until the train reached Brian's stop.

Immediately, Danny flicked open his paper and seethed. Hiding behind it, he pretended to read again.

● ● ●

The next day Danny got into the office almost an hour early. He'd hoped to beat Brian through the door but there he sat at the supervisor's desk scrawling on a note book in front of him. Brian lived alone, work was his life; Danny shouldn't have been surprised to find him sitting there already. Well, at least he'd seen that Danny was making an effort.

Danny beavered through his allotted tasks, and prepared his next day's work with his clients and suppliers. So far so good. And he had noticed Brian's eyes flick in his direction when he'd produced a flask and sandwich from his bag.

There was just an hour to go when Brian appeared at his side. "I see that you're practically up-to-date, Danny. That's good – really. But I'd hoped that if you were out of work, you'd have asked what else you could do."

"I was about to tidy my desk then do just that," said Danny quickly, hoping he sounded convincing.

"Well, I've saved you the trouble." Brian dumped a bulging file on Danny's desk. "I need you to check through these estimates. Refer to the new costings table where you need to. I need the updated figures for a meeting tomorrow."

That was a couple of hours work at least – and Brian knew it.

"One more thing," said Brian.

Not more surely!

"I've got your home phone number from your file," Brian waved a post-it note under Danny's nose. "I'll give you a call this evening – see how you got on."

"Sure," said Danny. *Make certain that I've stayed behind and finished the job.* Danny pulled the file towards him without further comment.

An hour-and-a-half later Brian went home. Danny didn't look up but he could see the laptop case swinging in Brian's hand.

After a further hour, Danny stretched and slammed the file closed, the sound echoing through the otherwise deserted office. Finished. Surely not even Brian could find fault with that.

Danny got to London Bridge with three minutes to spare before his next train – how's that for timekeeping! Perhaps this evening, what was left of it, wouldn't be so bad after all.

Danny's luck didn't last.

The train crawled through a couple of stations then stopped. After a further ten minute delay there was an announcement. Because of an incident this train would be terminating at the next station. Which it did.

Danny, along with a hundred other passengers, was turned out onto the platform to wait for some indication of what was going on. Three Bridges, he'd only got as far as Three Bridges. Eventually there was movement. The train Danny had been on now clanked out of the station – back towards London. Nothing, it seemed, would be travelling further down the line.

Danny swore under his breath. Now what? If only he had left on time – before the incident. Eventually 'the incident' was announced as a fatality down the line at Balcombe. Danny sighed, hardly the train company's fault then. Balcombe. Danny was sure there was something significant about that station, but he couldn't think what it was. He kicked at a stone on the platform. Still it could be worse – some poor sod had ended-up under a train.

From there it was a nightmare journey. A dilapidated bus was eventually organised stopping at Balcombe then Haywards Heath. From there a shuttle-train, trapped south of the incident, ferried passengers further down the line.

Finally Danny got home. Ten past nine! The whole evening wasted. He hadn't even taken off his jacket when the phone rang.

Brian, thought Danny. The last thing he needed. He snatched up the phone. "Yes?"

There was a slight pause, then a woman's carefully professional voice was explaining to him that she was a police officer and could he confirm his name.

Danny did so. "What's the matter?" he asked. "I haven't done anything wrong have I?"

"There has been an incident," explained the voice. "A fatality at Balcombe train station."

"Yeah, I know. All the trains were cocked-up. I've just got in from work."

47

"A man was killed," said the careful voice. "He had no identification..." she paused.

"And you're ringing me – because?" Suddenly Danny remembered why Balcombe had been familiar. That was the station Brian had got out at yesterday. "This man," he asked quickly. "Was he carrying a laptop?"

"He was," confirmed the policewoman. "And inside the case was a post-it note with your name and phone number."

Well, that was that. *Brian was the incident at Balcombe*. Poor sod. Silently Danny punched the air.

He gave the police all the information he could. He didn't know Brian's address, but now that they had a name the police could no doubt track it down. He told them that there'd be no one there anyway; Brian had lived alone – which was hardly a surprise.

"Oh, I just thought of something," said Danny. It was true, he hadn't worked it out beforehand, he was thinking on his feet. "The laptop," he said. "There's an important meeting tomorrow – and all the information we need is on that machine. There's no next-of-kin, the laptop is company property anyway, and I could drive round to pick it up in say half-an-hour." Danny was very persuasive; after all he *had* been helpful and indentified the body. Eventually it was agreed that he could sign for the laptop and use it for his important meeting.

By half-past-ten, Danny was back home with Brian's laptop plugged in, searching for his end-of-probation assessment. There it was. Danny read it, and re-read it. Borderline, Brian had said, and that was how it read. Danny was barely adequate in all categories – nothing glowing, but nothing damning either. Perhaps the deciding factor was to have been the expected phone call that evening. The phone call Brian wouldn't be making.

Danny hesitated, but then who would know? Step by step he altered his assessment. Borderline became brilliant, effort, attitude, yes even his timekeeping, was faultless. He saved the document, sat back - and had another thought. At this moment he was the only person who knew of Brian's death. There would have to be a re-shuffle of responsibilities now that Brian was gone. He scrolled back through the assessment. Here and there he added a comment that Danny should be considered for promotion, that he showed management potential. Why not? He saved the changes again and shut down the machine.

Despite his late night, Danny made an effort to get to work even earlier the next day. If he left the laptop under Brian's desk everyone would assume Brian had left it there himself. And, eventually, when Brian didn't turn up, someone would look on the machine for Danny's assessment. If necessary Danny would tell them that's where it would be, but it would be more convincing if they found it themselves.

Danny strode into the office and over to the supervisor's desk – and there sat Brian.

Danny gaped at him, unable to speak.

"Another early start, Danny. That's a good sign." Then Brian noticed the laptop case. For a moment he frowned, then a smile of realisation spread across his face. "The post-it note!" he said.

Danny still couldn't say anything.

"Someone found it and called your number. Is that what happened?"

Danny managed to nod.

"I was *almost* home," said Brian. "Then this thug ran past in a hood. He snatched the laptop and ran for it, back towards the station. Then he cut across a field towards the tracks; I thought it was lost for sure."

"It was stolen?" Danny was incredulous.

Brian raised an eyebrow. "Surely you don't think I'm so careless that I left it behind. Still, it was good of you, Danny, to make the effort to get it back for me." Brian patted the estimates file. "And after you'd stayed late to update these costings. That must have taken-up your whole evening."

Danny gave a dismissive shrug.

Brian settled back in his chair. "Your assessment was borderline, Danny – as I told you. But I think you've just proved yourself to be both honest and reliable. You deserve the benefit of the doubt." Brian nodded his approval. "Now, if you'll hand over my laptop, I'll amend your assessment accordingly."

First published in The Weekly News, 2011

Off the Shelf

by Linda Barrett

Bert Entwistle watched the pretty young woman as she made her way along the row of biscuits. She stopped and popped a packet of jam creams into her basket. He hovered at the end of the aisle. She moved on to the pet food. He followed. Bert wasn't fond of animals and he hoped she wouldn't linger. To his utter consternation she did, adding a tin of cat food to her items. He could feel a sneeze coming on.

She moved to the baked beans. The few left were at the back of the shelf and she couldn't quite reach them. Bert hurriedly replaced a tin of plum tomatoes he was pretending to look at and headed towards her. Too late! A gangly youth, who Bert recognised as Keith Docherty, the new shelf stacker, beat him to it.

"Can I help?" he heard him say.

She smiled at the young man. "Thank you so much," she said, pushing a wisp of blonde hair away from her left eye with one hand as she took the tin from him with the other.

Damn!

Keith Docherty beamed. "No probs. Is there anything else I can get for you?"

"Docherty!"

He spun round. "Yes, Mr Entwistle?"

"Have you finished unloading those dairy products yet?"

"No, Mr Entwistle."

"Then get off the shop floor and finish what I asked you to do."

"Yes, Mr Entwistle," he gave the woman an apologetic look and left the shop floor. Bert turned to his prey.

"Sorry about that," he crooned. "Can I be of any assistance?"

"No, I'm fine now," she gave him a little half smile and walked away. Bert decided it wouldn't do to follow her around the shop any more. She might accuse him of stalking her. She'd been in the supermarket before and she would no doubt be in again.

He was right. She was back the very next day and he spotted her as soon as she walked through the door. He watched discreetly as she filled her basket. When she'd finished she joined the end of the queue at checkout 6. Bert dashed around the back of the checkouts. Lil Turner was working on 6 and she was in the middle of serving a customer with an overflowing trolley.

"Just finish that customer and then go for your tea-break, Mrs. Turner, I'll take over."

"I've had my tea-break, thanks, Mr Entwistle," and she continued scanning.

"Well, you've been working hard and you're looking tired. Go and get a nice cup of tea."

Lil's jaw dropped in surprise but she finished serving the customer and went off to get a second tea-break.

Bert would ordinarily have considered the checkouts far beneath him but he scanned the shopping of the next two customers at speed. Finally it was her turn. He smiled at her and slowed considerably. "We meet again," he said. She looked confused. "You came in yesterday and had trouble reaching the baked beans."

"Ah, yes, I remember."

Bert cleared his throat and pushed his glasses further up his nose.

"Oh, I see you have a cat," he picked up a tin of cat food from the conveyer belt. "I love cats," he lied.

"Yes, me too, I have three."

Bert scratched his chest vigorously. He finished scanning her shopping and to his delight she paid by credit card, which meant he could see her name. Miss Deborah Green.

"Thank you, Miss Green." He cooed as he handed it back to her.

"You're the manager, aren't you?" she asked. "Please don't think I'm being forward but I don't suppose you have any jobs going? I've worked on a checkout before."

Bert couldn't believe his luck. He tried to keep his voice steady. "Could you come back this afternoon for an interview, say at two?"

"Yes, I can. Thank you. I'll see you then," and she was gone.

Bert had a light lunch and then helped himself to a packet of mint chewing gum from the shop floor to freshen his breath. At 1:50 he made his way to the front of the store and positioned himself by the door. She was on time.

"Ah! Miss Green! That's what I like to see, nice and punctual." He escorted her to his office. To his delight Deborah Green had quite a lot of experience working in supermarkets and she came with glowing references. He was just getting into his stride when the phone rang.

"Yes Julie, what is it?"

"I'm sorry to bother you, Mr Entwistle, but there's a policeman to see you about the missing electrical stock."

He sighed. "Okay, give me another five minutes then I'll see him."

"I'm very sorry about that Miss, er, Deborah. When can you start?"

"As soon as you like."

"Splendid, shall we say Monday then?" He felt tempted to ask her out for a drink there and then but he didn't want to scare her off. Best to wait a bit. Anyway he had this confounded policeman to see. He'd look forward to Monday.

It soon came around and once again she was punctual. Bert would have liked to have trained her himself but that would have been too obvious so he reluctantly handed her over to the supervisor on shift. He waited till lunch time and then decided to see how she was getting on. To his relief she'd been left alone for a short time. What's more, to add to his luck, the checkouts were very quiet and she had no customers for the moment. He hurried over. He was about half way across the floor when he saw a familiar figure approach her. Docherty! Bert arrived at the checkout just seconds after him.

"Docherty, why are you never where I've asked you to be?"

"Sorry, Mr Entwistle," and he hurried off.

"And how are we getting on Debbie? You don't mind if I call you Debbie?"

"Not at all," she smiled. "I'm fine. Everyone's been very helpful."

Encouraged by the smile he decided this was the time. He pushed his spectacles further up his nose, cleared his throat and leant over the checkout.

"I wonder, erm, Debbie, if you would consider having dinner with me this evening?"

"I'd be delighted," she said without hesitation. "In fact there's a new Italian restaurant opened in James Street that I'd like to try. I believe it's excellent. A bit expensive though I'm afraid."

"No problem Debbie, no problem at all. I'll see if I can get a booking. Shall we say eight o' clock?"

The booking was made and Bert arranged to pick her up at her place at 7:45. He spent the rest of the day in a state of blissful expectation.

Debbie was ready when he arrived and the evening went better than he could have ever dreamed. Over the meal the conversation got around to his bachelor pad.

"It sounds wonderful," she enthused. "I'd love to see it."

Bert cleared his throat and pushed his spectacles further up his nose. "Well, why don't we stop in at my place for a drink, It's on the way to yours."

"Okay, sounds great."

He paid the bill, the size of which would normally have given him indigestion. But he was in far too good a mood. He paid it gladly and they left.

"What would you like to drink?" Bert said as they entered his flat.

"Oh, red wine if you have it. Could I use your little girl's room?"

"Sure, it's at the end of the hall."

He got a bottle of wine from the rack and hunted around for the corkscrew. She was gone quite a while and Bert assumed she was making herself pretty for him. When she finally came back he thought she looked stunning. They drank their wine and chatted.

Bert reached for her hand. It was at this moment that the door bell rang. He sighed but decided he'd better answer it.

"Mr Entwistle?" enquired the man at the door. He was holding up a badge. "My name's Detective Sergeant Collins and this is Detective Constable Hopkins," he indicated to his companion. "May we come in?"

"I don't believe this. Do you know what time it is?"

"It shouldn't take long, Sir."

Bert reluctantly stood aside to allow them in.

"As you know Sir we're investigating the disappearance of a large amount of electrical stock from your store over the past few months."

"Can't this wait until tomorrow?"

"I'm afraid not, Sir. As I said it shouldn't take long. Would you mind if we had a look around? We do have a search warrant." Collins produced a piece of paper from his inside pocket and handed it to Bert. He then nodded to his colleague who left the room. Within minutes he was back indicating to the sergeant to follow him.

Bert paled and Debbie sat silently watching. The men returned.

"You seem to have rather a large amount of expensive electrical items in your spare room, Sir. Can you explain that?"

Bert just shook his head in bewilderment. "How did you know?"

"We had a tip off."

"From me," Debbie stood up as she spoke. I had a quick look round while you thought I was in the bathroom.

"You? Why?"

"Keith Docherty and I are store detectives. Head Office has suspected you of the thefts for some time so they sent us in to see what we could find. You really shouldn't have been so greedy, you know."

"Are you ready to go?" the voice came from the doorway. It was Docherty. Debbie went over and they put their arms around each other.

"You should also try going for women your own age. Still, I've got a feeling you'll have plenty of time to think about that where you're going."

JEAN'S BREAD PUDDING

by Rob Nisbet

The pavement outside the garden-of-rest gates was barely wide enough for the wheelchair, so Glenda took up her usual position behind her husband, Roy, as he pushed his father up the gentle hill towards the village.

Glenda saw Mr Frazer twist awkwardly in his chair to speak, his face sullen as usual. "Good choice of flowers, Son," he said. "Your mother would have liked them."

Roy shot a quick grin at Glenda, over his shoulder; he at least could still find some humour in the situation. "Glenda chose them, Dad," he said in an exaggerated loud voice. "She was quite insistent about the type she wanted – something colourful."

Glenda didn't expect any further response so wasn't surprised that her father-in-law turned back in his chair tucking-in the tartan blanket fussily round his waist, ignoring her again. Was this how it was going to be, every weekend from now on, visiting Roy's dad, doing his shopping, wheeling him up and down the hill to the cemetery, while she trudged along behind, last place in the procession?

It had been so different when Jean was alive. It was true, Glenda *had* selected the flowers with care. She wanted something with big blooms, bright colours, something cheerful. That was how she would always remember her mother-in-law, larger than life, always jolly, despite her illness, always ready for a chat and a chuckle.

"Glenda," she'd said at practically their first meeting. "You must call me Mum." Call me Mum! How that had embarrassed Roy at the time! But somehow his mother had known that Glenda would be the one he'd settle down with. And she'd been right of course.

Glenda could still remember the first time she had met Jean. Roy had introduced her to a slightly plump, smiling woman, her grey-streaked hair held back by a teenage alice-band – practical but unflattering. Jean was baking, her hands and apron were covered in flour and the side of her nose was smeared with pastry. Quite unconcerned about her appearance, Jean had offered Glenda a kitchen chair and in no time they'd been chatting like old friends.

Roy parked the wheelchair at the entrance to the village teashop. This had become a ritual, this stop for coffee and cake on the way home.

"Let me help you, Mr Frazer," said Glenda offering her father-in-law an arm.

"I can manage," Mr Frazer snapped, waving Glenda away like an annoying bluebottle. "Let me walk these few steps at least – while I still can."

They settled themselves at a neat little table in the bay window and ordered three coffees and a selection of homemade cakes. Glenda was glad of the rest, and of the warmth that seeped its way into her walking boots, making her realise how chilly the day was outside. Perhaps it was her accountant's training but she found herself automatically adding up her and Roy's share of the bill. Mr Frazer would always pay for this little treat. She'd never heard him say thank you; it was his way of saying that he appreciated them coming over to see him. It worked out at a couple of pounds each. She felt vaguely that Mr Frazer was buying their time and attention, and at these prices he was getting a bargain.

Glenda became aware that an awkward silence had crept over them: another impossibility when Jean had been around. Jean had always been so friendly, so interested in other people.

The coffees arrived with a two-tier cake-stand. Both levels held a selection of cakes; there were sugar-dusted sponges, almond fingers, meringues and a chunk of bread pudding.

"What would Glenda like, Roy?" enquired Mr Frazer. This was his treat and he liked to oversee the allocation of the cakes.

Glenda gave her husband a mutinous look. "Oh, don't worry about me, Mr Frazer," she said, as if he had spoken directly to her. "I'm not feeling that hungry." She deliberately turned to stare out of the window, at the busy little street, bright in the winter sunshine. But her own mood was far from sunny. She would let Roy visit his dad alone from now on. The old man probably wouldn't even notice she was missing.

☕ ☕ ☕

Between them, Roy and his father had eaten most of the cakes. Mr Frazer senior prodded the block of bread pudding suspiciously. "Do you remember, Roy, the bread puddings your mother used to make? She had her own recipe. I gave that to you didn't I?"

Roy nodded. His mother's hand-written recipe had been handed over like some treasured heirloom – not to Glenda who might have made some use of it, but to Roy, who had shoved it in a kitchen drawer then forgotten about it. Roy could see a faraway look in his father's eyes. Thoughts of Jean would make him maudlin and depressed, and he was hardly the life and soul at the best of times.

"She used black treacle," said Mr Frazer to his son. His voice had got quieter, his old grey eyes wistful and unfocused. "That was her secret. And she would pound the soaked bread with the potato masher. Do you remember? She used to let you do that part, when you were a young lad. There were never any lumps, always smooth and no dry bready pieces either."

"It's looking a little brighter outside," lied Roy, anxious to stem the melancholy. "We're done here aren't we? It's time we got you home."

❦❦❦

I know he's your father," said Glenda, over supper that night, "so naturally you feel obliged to visit – but really there's no need for me to go too. He barely even acknowledges that I'm there."

"That's just his way," said Roy dismissively. "He never was a very sociable person. Mum always said that she was jolly enough for the two of them." Roy leant his elbows on the table. "She was always interested in people, you see, while he was content to read the newspaper. That meant that Mum was the one who had all the friends. Remember that mountain of sympathy cards? Dad was happy enough just being 'Jean's husband', having friends by association. But now of course he's quite alone. He depends on us for shopping and a bit of human contact."

"Then he should try to be less of a grumpy old man," said Glenda. "And it's not only me who thinks so. While you were helping him into the house today, I had a quick chat with his neighbour. She's about his age, and a widow. She asked me how he was, how he was coping without Jean."

"What did you say?"

"Well, he'd just spent the afternoon ignoring me, so I told her how miserable he was being. And *she* agreed. She was a good friend of Jean's, and was always popping round for tea and a gossip. She's almost afraid to speak to him now in case she upsets him even more. The thing they had in common was Jean, and now she's gone, there's no connection. If you ask me, Jean's left *her* a bit lonely too."

Roy nodded. "I know how she feels," he said. "Every time Dad mentions Mum at all, he gets *that* look, introspective and sad. I keep having to change the subject. I miss her too, you know. What's it been now, two months? He's still adjusting to life without her. Give him some more time, eh Glen? Come down with me next Saturday."

Glenda was silent for a moment, then she returned Roy's cheeky grin. "Okay, you win," she said. "But do we have to go to the cemetery every week? I don't think it does him any good, it just reminds him more of what he's lost."

Roy agreed. "And then I wouldn't have to stuff myself with all those little pink sponge cakes in the tea shop."

"I know!" said Glenda brightly. "Fetch that recipe he's always going on about. Next Saturday, we'll do his shopping on the way, then we'll have coffee and cake at his place. Break the routine, with Jean's bread pudding."

"Worth a try," said Roy.

Glenda poured boiling water on the sultanas. It would make them juicier – according to Jean's recipe. She had the ingredients spread out in front of her, including a gleaming new tin of black treacle and a large pot of mixed spice.

Carefully, Glenda cut the crusts from the bread, then broke the slices into a bowl of milk to soak. Then she reached for the potato masher. Glenda could imagine Jean, in her apron, cheerfully pounding at the soggy bread till she produced a consistent sludge.

Glenda sighed. If that's what Jean's recipe demanded, that's what she'd do. She hoped Mr Frazer would appreciate it; at least she was making an effort.

On Saturday, Glenda carried her tray of bread pudding, cut into blocky fingers, through to Mr Frazer's kitchen table. Roy bustled to and fro, bringing in the bags of shopping.

"Oh no!" he said as he brought in the final bag. "I've forgotten the bread." Roy turned to his father who had shuffled into the kitchen behind them. "Dad, you just sit here, I've got to pop out again to the shop. Won't be long. And Glenda's got something to show you."

Glenda's eyes were wide and she shook her head slightly at her husband. *You can't just leave me alone with him like this.*

Roy spread out his hands and shrugged. "I'll be as quick as I can," he said and dashed out.

Mr Frazer walked slowly to the kitchen table and sat down. He hadn't said anything and seemed to be avoiding Glenda's eye. Then he noticed the foil covered tray.

"Speaking of bread," said Glenda brightly, as if she hadn't noticed the short silence, "I've made you some bread pudding. And I used Mum's – Jean's – recipe." Suddenly Glenda thought this wasn't such a good idea after all. Using Jean's recipe – it sounded wrong, irreverent, like she'd been caught wearing Jean's shoes.

Mr Frazer lifted the foil cover. "You made this for me?" he asked.

Glenda said that she had, quickly justifying herself by adding that it would make a change from going to the teashop again. "I followed the recipe exactly. You know, treacle, spices and the potato masher."

Mr Frazer looked up. "Jean always insisted on mashing the bread," he said. "And she was right – nobody's bread pudding tasted as good as Jean's."

"I imagined her," said Glenda. "While I was following her recipe, reading her hand writing. It was as if she were by my side, guiding me through each process. I don't mean anything spooky – just memories."

Mr Frazer was nodding. "I know exactly what you mean," he said. "Jean was so much a part of my life, that I still feel her, here in the house, in every little household task."

Glenda saw then what Roy had described as 'that look' spreading over her father-in-law's face. Yes he looked sad and a bit tearful, but at least he was talking to her. "It can't be easy," she said sympathetically. "You were together a long time."

"Forty-two years, three months," he said instantly, "You can tell, I've been counting."

Glenda gave a slight smile. "She was certainly a character. Easy to talk to, and a good listener too." Glenda noticed a single tear crawl down the furrows of her father-in-law's face. She reached across to him, offering him a paper square of kitchen towel.

Mr Frazer accepted it gratefully, wiping at his eyes and nose. "Thank you," he said. "Oh, not for the tissue. Thank you for not changing the subject. Nobody talks to me about Jean any more. I suppose they think I'll get distressed – well I suppose I will, now and then, but not mentioning her is like denying she ever existed. She was the biggest part of my life but now even my own son can't seem to talk about her."

"Roy just doesn't want to upset you, and, I think talking about her upsets him a bit too at the moment. He hides that of course. Changing the subject makes it easier for him to cope as well."

So, thought Glenda, *there's* a twist. Mr Frazer wasn't miserable because people spoke about Jean, but because they avoided talking about her.

Mr Frazer dabbed at his eyes again. "People talk of their wives or husbands as their other half. Well, with us, Jean was *more* than half. I didn't seem to have a full life of my own; I was a portion of Jean. She was so vibrant, so alive; I did little more than tag along, content to be in her shadow. And I'm beginning to realise what I've been missing." He reached across the table and lightly touched Glenda's hand. "Even you, Glenda," he said, "my own daughter-in-law, I've hardly spoken to you except through Jean, and then through Roy. Forgive me; I don't have Jean now to make the first move. I've got to learn again how to get to know people by myself." He sniffed and gave himself a little shake. "Now then, how about some coffee and bread pudding?"

Roy came in clutching a loaf of bread and stood amazed in the kitchen doorway. Glenda was laughing at something his father had said, some embarrassing tale of when Roy was a young boy. She'd tease him about that later, no doubt.

"Roy," called his father, "come and taste this bread pudding. It's every bit as good as your mother used to make."

"I had a good teacher," said Glenda.

Roy sat at the table and, after a while, joined in the reminiscing. Yes he could see that his father was a bit tearful but, strangely, this was also the happiest Roy had seen him since they'd lost Mum; he was more alive now than he had been for several years. And yes, Glenda's bread pudding, his mother's recipe, was very good indeed.

Mr Frazer let his smile drop for a moment. He spoke to Glenda. "You've done me a power of good today, Glenda," he said. "Thank you. And I wonder, next week, could you make another bread pudding? There's a neighbour, next door, she used to come round to see Jean and was very fond of her cakes. She's a widow and I imagine she's feeling Jean's loss too. I'd like to invite her round, see how she is."

Glenda smiled to herself. "A good idea, Mr Frazer. I'm sure there must be a lot of people who'd like to talk over old times and memories. It's just the sort of thing Jean would do."

"There's one more thing you can do for me, Glenda," said her father-in-law. "Please, call me Dad."

First published in Woman's Weekly, 2006

Something's Bothering Bill

by Linda Barrett

Bill hauled the ladder into the back garden. His face puce with effort he finally got it in place on the lawn and opened it up. His wife, Eileen, followed him out.

"What on earth are you doing?"

"I'm going to find out what that new bloke, next-door-but-one, has got in his back garden. He's been building something, I know that much. I didn't like the look of him when I watched him moving in. He's very shifty if you ask me."

Eileen sighed resignedly.

Bill heaved himself up the ladder, his knees complaining vehemently at every step.

"Why did Tom, next door, have to put up a six foot fence anyway? We used to be able to see into every garden in the street."

"It could have had something to do with you hosing down his barbecue," said Eileen.

"He asked for that. Bloomin' barbecues every day. All that smoke."

"They weren't every day and I don't think you should have turned the hose on it. He'd paid a lot for those steaks."

"Steaks, my foot! Glorified burgers, they were. Then Rob and Marie put a high fence up on the other side. *We'd just like some privacy,*" Bill mimicked.

"I wonder why?" said Eileen. And shaking her head she went indoors.

Reaching the top of the ladder Bill could at last see into all the back gardens. None of the other neighbours had gone for high fences. Funny that.

Something had been going on next-door-but-one ever since the new neighbour moved in. He didn't know what it was but he would find out.

Ah, something had definitely been built there but he couldn't quite see what it was. He squinted as hard as he could but he still couldn't make it out.

Very slowly he lowered himself down to the ground. He went back indoors to get his binoculars from the living room window sill.

Five minutes later he started his ascent again. This one made even more arduous by the binoculars dangling round his neck and banging against his chest. Finally, he was there. He raised the binoculars to his eyes and aimed them at the new structure in his neighbour's garden.

He leant against the ladder while he focused. Yes, he could see it now. It was some sort of pen. Bill dreaded to think what kind of animals would be going inside it? They could attract vermin. Maybe he should get up a petition.

Just then a figure came into view. "Can I help you with something?" shouted his next-door-but-one neighbour.

The start it gave Bill was so violent that he caused the ladder, which was balancing precariously on an uneven lawn, to shake uncontrollably. It finally toppled, crashing to the ground and taking Bill with it.

***

A few days later, Bill, with his leg in plaster, was sitting at the living room window, binoculars in hand, watching the comings and goings of his street. He was momentarily distracted by Eileen asking him if he wanted a cup of tea and so he was surprised when the doorbell rang.

Eileen went to answer it.

"A visitor for you," she called from the hall. Now he was really surprised. Bill never got visitors. Then, to his amazement, in walked the next-door-but-one neighbour.

"Hello Bill! I just thought I'd come and see how you were getting on. I felt bad about the accident. I didn't mean to startle you," he said, turning a small box round awkwardly in his hands. "Anyway, I've brought you some eggs, nice and fresh from my own chickens. The name's Eddie by the way." Eddie held out his hand.

"Oh! Very enterprising," said Bill and his face lit up as he leaned across and took the box of eggs. "Eileen heard from Tom, next door, you were getting chickens. Nosey old so and so that. Doesn't miss a darn thing. That chicken pen's a real beauty, by the way. Would you like a cup of tea?"

"Don't mind if I do," said Eddie. "So, tell me more about this Tom. Is he married or does he live on his own?"

"Put the kettle on, Eileen. Eddie and I are going to have a nice, neighbourly chat."

Just a Very Small Slice of Cake

by Rob Nisbet

"Surprise!"

At first Tina didn't know what to say. There on the landing stood a tiny woman wrapped head-to-toe in a riot of fluffy knitting. It took her a few moments to realise that somewhere deep in the multi-coloured wool was the little white-haired figure of her Aunt. "Aunty Maureen, how nice to see you." Tina drew back from the doorway to allow her aunt into the hall. "Come in won't you; Kevin was just about to put the kettle on."

Maureen gathered-up several shopping bags and made her way into her niece's flat. "Don't worry about the kettle," she said cheerfully, waving her bags as she scuttled down the hallway, "I've bought a few provisions with me." Her thin lips curved into a smile and her eyes twinkled back in Tina's direction. "In fact," she said, "I've done a very wicked thing, and I want the two of you to help me consume the evidence."

At these words Kevin's cheeky grin appeared from the living room. "Hello Aunt Maureen. Cold out is it?" He gave her the required peck on the cheek and managed to stop himself commenting on the garish mauves and greens of the woollen coat and hat that Maureen was shrugging herself out of. "Sounds like you've been shoplifting, is that it? You've got a bag of illegal buns for us to eat before the police catch up with you."

Aunt Maureen placed her bags next to the coffee table then perched herself on the edge of the sofa arranging the bright gold and orange folds of her dress about her knees. Out of her voluminous coat she was a tiny woman stick thin in a brittle bird-like way. But her grey-blue eyes were keen and bright behind her glasses. They flicked quickly round the room.

Oh Lord, thought Tina. She's looking for that hideous vase she bought us for Christmas. Tina smiled at her aunt and wished she could somehow signal to Kevin – *whatever you do, don't mention the vase.*

Aunt Maureen's eyes came to rest finally on Kevin as he sat down across the room. "Not exactly shoplifting," she said. "Though I admit that I have been very wicked. Tina dear, you're looking very thin; I've always thought that you should eat a bit more. Would you fetch some small plates, oh and some wine glasses – then I'll tell you what I've done."

Tina and Kevin exchanged a quick glance as if to ask each other what was going on. Tina gave a small shrug and popped out to the kitchen.

Aunt Maureen placed the contents of her bags on the coffee table one by one. "Wine, Chocolates and a delicious looking cake," she said. "Kevin dear, would you open the wine? I find corkscrews these days just too fiddly for these old hands of mine. Ah Tina, the glasses – plain I see, but serviceable."

Tina turned one of the slender stemmed glasses round between her fingers. "I like these," she said.

"Oh I don't mean to criticise," said Aunt Maureen quickly. "I've been told far too often that my tastes can be somewhat - gaudy. People of my age tend to dress in safe blues or grey and everything they own is traditional and boring. I prefer something more cheerful. I have a set of glasses at home, pink glass with a raised raspberry design round the rim. I think they're splendid but they always raise an eyebrow when I have guests. Now then, Tina dear, perhaps you could open the chocolates, cellophane wrappers are so shiny I can never see the edges properly."

Tina quickly unwrapped the chocolate box; they were her favourites, from Belgium — all pralines and creamy centres. She unfolded the gold foil lining and offered one to her aunt.

"How kind, Tina. I'll just have this small one here in the corner, then it won't spoil the display too much. Help yourselves you two. It's a vital part of my plan, that these chocolates get eaten."

Kevin had opened the wine and was reading the label. He had commented to Aunt Maureen once that this was a wine he liked. She had obviously remembered, and it was nicely chilled too. "So," he said, "if you didn't steel these delights — what's this dreadful crime you've committed?"

"Just a half glass for me please," said Aunt Maureen as Kevin began to pour. "I do like to see a bottle opened don't you? Once a bottle or a box is opened you can just sit back and work your way through it."

Tina and Kevin each took a chocolate from the box and sat down with a glass of wine, still not quite sure what was going on. Aunt Maureen may have eccentric tastes but she seemed to them to be the most unlikely of criminals; she was, for a start, hardly inconspicuous. Just what was she about to tell them?

"Now then," Aunt Maureen leant forward conspiratorially. "My crime. It all started with that lovely vase I bought you for Christmas…"

Tina and Kevin's eyes met in a brief moment of panic, but Tina was ready: "Oh Kevin, I meant to tell you. Sally across the landing, she asked to borrow that vase. She said it would be perfect for some blue and orange flowers she had."

Kevin was impressed. As an explanation it sounded plausible and Tina had been so quick that Aunt Maureen would probably accept it without question.

"Anyway," Aunt Maureen continued, "I was passing the window of the Help the Aged shop in the high street when I saw a vase very similar to yours. So I went in. It had the original box and packaging but the really curious thing was that these vases are hand made — each one is supposed to be unique but it reminded me so much of your one that I was tempted to buy it for you – then you'd have a pair!"

"What a lovely thought," said Tina absently reaching for another chocolate. "Isn't that nice, Kevin?"

"Yeah, lovely," Kevin took a sip of wine. "But what is this wicked thing you've done?"

"Well, I bought the vase, box and all, good as new – and for only a pound!" Aunt Maureen chuckled to herself. "Can you believe it? What a bargain. I know, of course, how much they fetch in a department store. In fact I still had the original till receipt in my handbag. And that's my crime. Without a second thought I took the charity shop vase straight back to the store I bought yours from - I had the original packing and a receipt - and they gave me a full refund there and then." Aunt Maureen's eyes fell to where her fingers played with the folds of her dress. "I had to tell them, I'm afraid, that I'd bought the vase as a gift but that it wasn't to the taste of those I'd bought it for."

Tina had the grace to turn a shade of embarrassed red. "Oh, Aunt Maureen…" she began.

"I know, I know," Maureen interrupted quickly. "I've never known myself do anything like it before. It was so easy, but so very wicked. My poor old heart was all of a flutter. It gave me a bit of a thrill if I'm honest – which I always try to be. But I don't think I'll be turning to a life of crime – not at my age."

Kevin grinned at the idea – Aunt Maureen: master criminal.

Tina still didn't fully understand. "So why the cake and chocolates and wine?"

"I just felt, Tina dear, that you should have something from my ill-gotten gains. After all I did get the charity shop vase with the intention of you having a pair. Cut the cake would you Tina dear, I'll just slide it out of its fancy box."

Tina did as instructed; it was a moist fruit cake with a rich fondant topping. "It looks delicious."

"That's good," said Aunt Maureen. "I wanted to be sure of getting something you'd *really* like. Just a very small slice of cake for me please." Aunt Maureen took the slice of cake and placed the plate carefully on the table next to her one chocolate and half-glass of wine. "I do like to see a cake started, don't you?" Aunt Maureen smiled fondly at Tina and Kevin and an extra twinkle appeared in her shrewd eyes. "And once a cake is cut," she said, "even if you still have the box, you can't really give it away or take it back to the shop. You'll just have to eat it all yourselves, won't you?"

First published in My Weekly, 2010

The Children's Car Park

by Linda Barrett

"Where's Terry this morning?" asked a breathless young woman, as she approached the reception desk. She was pushing a small boy in a buggy.

"I honestly don't know Mrs Hargreaves. You must be about the tenth person to ask. I suppose he must be off sick. We haven't been told anything."

"The barrier's down. We've had to park miles away. Both your other car parks are full."

Eileen apologised yet again and Jayne Hargreaves took her seat in the waiting room.

The Paediatric Unit at St Mary's was housed in its own building adjacent to the main hospital. In 1992 everyone had been surprised and delighted when the local council turned the large area of wasteland, behind the building, into a low cost car park. It was specifically designated for the use of their patients' escorts and was referred to by staff and parents alike as The Children's Car Park.

Eileen had been working there when it had opened. Terry had arrived and a barrier had been erected. This was quickly followed by a little hut for him to use in inclement weather.

The day finally came to an end and Eileen had lost track of how many people she'd had to apologise to for the closure of their car park.

The next day the first patient to come into the clinic was Mrs Platt with her five year old daughter, Daisy. She was only just on time, which was unusual.

"Why is the car park closed?" she asked.

"Oh, not again! I don't know, Mrs Platt, but I think we'll have to ring the council today and find out. Terry wasn't here yesterday either."

It was a very busy morning but as soon as she had a minute Eileen rang her boss Simon Anderson.

"The patients are complaining that the car park's closed again. Do you think we should ring the council?"

"Okay, I have a meeting in a moment but I'll ring later. In the meantime explain to them that the car park is actually nothing to do with us. It's a council car park."

"I know. The trouble is people take it for granted now and a flat rate of £1 is incredibly cheap for hospital parking."

"Convenient too," agreed Simon.

"And Terry's well liked by the patients. Have you seen the amount of booze he gets at Christmas?"

Again Simon agreed and promised he would do his best to sort it out.

It was 5pm before he showed up in reception.

"No news about the car park, I'm afraid. I've been on to the council all afternoon. They've passed me to so many different departments I'm dizzy. No one seems to know anything about it. They say as far as they're concerned the car park's ours."

"That's ridiculous," said Eileen, "Someone must know something. They've been running it for over twenty years."

"Yes, and employing Terry, of course. If I don't get any joy tomorrow I'll ring their personnel department and see if they can tell me when Terry's coming back."

Eileen was just about to go to lunch, the next day, when Simon came into the reception office. He looked puzzled.

"What's up?" she asked.

"I'm not sure. I've been on to the council again and still couldn't get any answers so I rang their personnel department.

75

They say they've never heard of Terry. They say that they've never employed anyone to work in our car park."

Some weeks later Eileen and Simon sat in the pub and reflected on the mystery that was Terry. Following numerous complaints about the closure of the car park the council had decided to re-open it. It turned out to be very lucrative for them and Dave Hanley, who took over from Terry, finally had a job after more than three years of unemployment. Best of all the patients had their cheap, convenient car park back again.

Eileen raised her glass for a toast. "Cheers Terry, wherever you might be!"

On a beach in Marbella Terry was sunning himself while sipping on a glass of sangria. He couldn't believe he'd had that brainwave, never mind getting away with it for all those years. It'd been so easy. The land was crying out to be used. The hospital thought he had been employed by the council and visa versa. What an earner. The initial layout for the barrier and hut had been well worth it. It had given him some credibility, so to speak. He felt he'd also provided a good service. Always friendly but never letting anyone know anything about himself. Now all he had to do was to relax and enjoy the rest of his life in the sun.

RESCUE LINE

by Rob Nisbet

Old Cody stood next to his juddering engine on the dark station platform. He was waiting, still as a statue, while around him the storm raged whipping-up dead leaves and wet newspapers, hurling them along the platform under the swaying string of bulbs that struggled to light the otherwise empty station.

At last a figure burst onto the platform by the closed ticket office, a young man, eyes screwed up against the lashing rain. He was dressed in dark green medical fatigues drenched almost black and lugged a large plastic case with a Red Cross symbol on its side.

Seeing Cody, the young man hurried forward pushing against the wind. "Is this train for St. Grays?" he shouted into the driving rain. "There's been an accident. And you're my last hope of getting there."

"An accident you say." Cody's voice was strong but slow, each syllable drawn out by his local Cornish accent. "I thought as much."

"Listen," the young man interrupted. "I don't have much time. There's been a mud slide and there's a woman trapped under a fallen wall. Can you get me there or not?"

"This train ain't been down to St. Grays for many a year." Cody glanced down the track, into the salt tainted fury of wind and rain. "But I reckon I could get you there. Is only one stop to

St. Grays, no signals. We'd have to go slow, mind. The weather can be a demon in these parts."

The young man nodded his agreement, "Tell me about it!"

Cody held open the door to the driver's cabin and gestured for the younger man to clamber inside with his case before seating himself heavily at the driver's seat. The cabin was cramped but the confined space was a welcome respite from the foul weather outside. The engine was already idling and in a matter of moments they were moving forward directly into the rain.

The young man threw down his medical case with a gasp of relief. He flicked his wet fringe out of his eyes and held out a damp hand in greeting. "What a night!" he said. "I'm Stewart, and – well, thanks for the lift."

"Cody," said Cody. His right hand pulled back steadily on the power handle. "You a doctor then?"

"Paramedic," Stewart corrected. "There are trees down on every road. The ambulance can't get through. The radio's dead, the land lines are down, even the mobiles aren't working." He lowered his hand, unshaken. "We hadn't gone far past the station, so I left Paul with the ambulance and thought I'd try for a train. And by some great good fortune there you were, Mr Cody, as if you were waiting for me."

"Just Cody," said Cody. "Don't mind do you lad, if I take off my arm?"

Stewart was too stunned to say anything as Cody shrugged loose his left arm and, with his right hand, placed it in front of him above a row of gauges.

"It's false," said Cody bluntly. "To be honest it can get a bit heavy an' irritating."

"I see..." said Stewart. "Hand and lower arm. What happened?"

Cody kept his eyes staring straight ahead into the night, scanning the barely visible tracks at each ineffectual swipe of the windscreen wipers. "A night just like this," he said. "Must be twenty-five years ago. You'd be too young, lad. But it were in all the papers back then. The bridge between here an' St. Grays collapsed. They say the river were in flood, that an' the storm bought the bridge down. Seventeen lives was lost that night. Seventeen young kids."

Stewart blew out his cheeks. "And you - were you driving the train?"

Cody nodded. "It were too dark, too wet to see. And my eyes were better then than now." He kept his attention on the way ahead, staring through his own reflection, as if forcing the train on by sheer effort of will. "Seventeen kids on a school outing. The track just fell away. There were only the one carriage. It slid and rolled down the bank, got itself stuck on the rocks at the river's edge. There was only two survivors; me, an' the school teacher. We was thrown free you see. I got crushed somehow, down the left side. They found Meg hours later screaming for help, clinging to the rock face. I were the lucky one; I lost an arm, poor Meg lost her mind."

"Just a minute!" Stewart reached into an inside pocket of his soaked jacket, fishing out a sheet of paper. "I thought so. We didn't get much of an incident report before the phones failed." He scanned the paper. "St. Grays – Market Street – woman under a collapsed wall, and a name, Meg. Just Meg, no surname."

Cody nodded sagely. "I knew it would be her."

"How?" Stewart was intrigued. "How could you possibly know it would be Meg?"

"Call it intuition." Cody reached across to the air brake on the left hand side, slowing the engine to a crawl. "We're coming up to the bridge." The rain pounded against the front window obscuring the way ahead.

Stewart leant closer to the glass as the single windscreen wiper swept back and forth, but he soon gave up. "Lucky you don't need to steer," he said. "I can't see a thing."

Cody kept facing forwards while his false arm rocked gently with the train's motion. "Take a look out the side then, lad. If you've got a head for heights."

Stewart looked out through the rain striped window. The dark night extended down sickeningly, sucking at his perceptions, dragging them screaming out over the sheer drop down to the surging river and rocks far below. Stewart swore and pulled back sharply. A further gust of wind hurled a wave of rain across the window with a shriek like screams of terror.

"Them kids didn't stand a chance," said Cody. "Not in a place like this. I got thrown onto the opposite bank, Meg clung to the rocks halfway down, screaming with grief she were, exhausted, barely hanging on. She were buoyed-up she says by the souls of the children, supporting her till help came."

"That's some trauma. You say it affected her mind?"

"Many hearts was broken that night," said Cody. "Almost everyone in St. Grays had lost a child of their own or of someone they knew. Meg though, she lost seventeen. The kids all adored their teacher, almost as much as she'd adored them. It broke her; she didn't work from that day, couldn't face the classroom..."

Cody's voice trailed away, lost in memory. Then he coughed and shook himself as if trying to shake his mind free of the past.

"She's the same age as me; no more than a slip of a girl back then, now she's almost fifty. Spends her days wandering the streets and cliff paths, talking to herself. The town looks after her though. As I said, she were well liked."

"Poor woman." Stewart squinted through the constant spattering of rain on the window. He thought it was clearing slightly; the tracks had re-appeared in front of them, faint stripes caught in the train's lights. "Let's hope we're in time. Is it much further?"

"Not far now." Cody raised the stump of his arm towards his face. "You're a medical man," he said. "Explain how it is I can still feel my fingers, after all these years."

"That's phantom limb syndrome," Stewart's eyes were drawn again to the slow rocking of the false arm. "The perception of your arm is so hard-wired into your brain that you feel it's still there. I've known cases where a patient can feel great pains in their foot, but with no foot or even a leg there to treat."

"And when I want to scratch my nose," Cody continued, raising his stump again, "I think about moving my fingers and the itch just vanishes. How'd you explain that?"

Stewart laughed shaking his head. "That's something you don't get taught at med-school."

Cody turned to look at him, their eyes locked just for a moment. "I guess if you want something badly enough," he said, "it just happens – however impossible it may be."

Cody pulled hard on the air brakes as the station slid into view around them. There were no lights and the ramshackle buildings looked like they hadn't been used in years. A figure stood on the dark platform picked out by the train lights; a man in his mid thirties, his mack running with water, waving at them through the rain, trying to attract their attention. Cody brought the engine to a stop next to where the man was standing. "That's Ryan," he said. "I know most people round these parts."

Ryan pulled open the door, instantly it caught the wind sending a chilling rush of air curling through the driver's cab. He nodded to Cody. "I knew you wouldn't get the train through for anyone else," he shouted above the wind. "But because it's her..."

"This here's the doctor," Cody bustled Stewart and his case out into the rain. "How is she?"

Ryan's face was grim. "Pretty bad. My car's through here Doc. We'll reach her in a couple of minutes."

Stewart threw his wet case into the back as Cody sat in the passenger seat resting his false arm on his lap. Ryan started up the engine and roared away from the station, the rain twinkling like glass needles in the headlights. Ryan glanced across at Cody. "Lord knows what we'll do with the train – now it's this side of the river."

Ryan handed Stewart a steaming mug of coffee. "You did good tonight, Doc. Thanks."

Stewart's bones felt steeped in cold. They had reached Meg just in time. Any longer and she may not have survived the freezing rain, never mind the wall that had slid on top of her. It seemed like the whole town had been there, in the dark with torches, scraping away at the wall brick-by-brick, trying to free the shivering woman trapped beneath.

Meg was upstairs now, in Ryan's bed. Ryan's wife, Cody and half-a-dozen other townsfolk were keeping an eye on her. She was sleeping, sedated, and her right leg was held rigid in a temporary splint.

Stewart took a scalding sip of the coffee feeling its warmth slip down inside him. "She'll be OK for the moment," he said, "till we can get her to a proper hospital. You know, I'm still amazed at how many people turned out to help."

Ryan shrugged. "People round here would do anything for Meg. You heard about the train crash I guess, and what happened to her?" He smiled. "You can't be around old Cody more than five minutes without him trotting out the day-the-bridge-collapsed story. I think he fancied her back then you know; the train driver and the school teacher."

Stewart sighed, thankful to be dry and warm at last, but now that he had time to sit and think, there were several things that didn't quite fit into place. And an image of Cody's arm rocking slowly to the movement of the train nagged, like an itch he couldn't scratch, at the back of his mind.

"I was in her class," said Ryan distractedly. "Back then, Meg was my teacher. I would have been one of her kids on that school outing too, but she sent me home. I'd got the beginnings of flu, but I struggled into school 'cause of the trip." He raised his eyes as if to the figure lying in his bed upstairs. "She sent me home."

"How come you were waiting at the station for us?" Stewart asked.

"I did it for Meg," said Ryan. "It was the only way of help getting through to her – so I waited, just in case."

Stewart took another sip of his coffee. "Why do I have the feeling that there's more to this? There's definitely something creepy about that driver."

"Cody? He's harmless. And he got you here didn't he? That's the main thing, with a bit of help."

"But he knew things… He was at the train station waiting with the engine running. He said he had an intuition that Meg had been hurt. And, did you know he has phantom feelings in his missing arm? It's spooky."

Ryan looked amused. "Oh Cody's flesh and blood alright. He may call it intuition; he's just more attuned to them than the rest of us I suppose."

Stewart was confused. "Attuned to who?"

"To the children," said Ryan. "It was Meg's school kids that carried you here. The bridge that collapsed twenty-five years ago has never been re-built."

First published in The Weekly News, 2008

The Good Samaritan

by Linda Barrett

Tom glanced at the illuminated petrol gauge. It was virtually on empty. Damn! It was the early hours of the morning and the twin beams of his headlights showed he was still in the middle of nowhere. And he had another two hours' driving to do in order to reach home. The only company he had was the radio. The 2 o'clock news was just starting.

"We are just receiving reports from the police that a category one prisoner has escaped from the high security wing at the Hammond Psychiatric Hospital. A spokesman for the hospital says that he cannot emphasise enough how dangerous this patient is and should not be approached under any circumstances...."

Tom switched the radio off before the bulletin had ended. He didn't want to be spooked on top of everything else. All the same he hit the central locking button to secure the doors.

He drove on and was relieved to see the lights of a garage just as he rounded a bend, about a mile on.

He pulled the black mini onto the forecourt, filled up and went inside. He grabbed a coffee and a sandwich and paid the attendant.

As Tom was making his way back to his car the lights went out inside the station. He'd barely got in his car when the guy who'd served him came out and locked up. He was driving away before Tom had taken the first bite of his sandwich. That was lucky, he thought. Another five minutes I'd have been too late. Wouldn't want to be stranded in the middle of nowhere and out of fuel with some maniac on the loose!

He relocked the doors then took a sip of the coffee. It was good and it warmed him. He was feeling tired despite the caffeine. He finished his snack and decided to lean back in his seat and take a nap, just for an hour or so, before continuing on his journey.

The piercing screams jolted him from his sleep. Without stopping to think he leapt out of the car and peered into the darkness. She came from nowhere, running and stumbling into the forecourt. She was screaming hysterically.

Tom ran to her. He grabbed her and held her until she calmed down.

Finally she spoke. "A man," she pointed frantically into the darkness. "I, I broke down. He, he came out of the d, darkness. Tried to get in the car." She started to sob again.

"Come on, get in my car. I won't hurt you."

She was clearly reluctant but, as Tom reasoned, the poor girl didn't have much choice. She'd obviously had one scare but she was forced to trust him. He gently eased her into the passenger seat, went around to the driver's side and got in himself. Once again he locked the doors.

"I'll phone the police," he said. He picked up his mobile. "No signal. Damn!"

"Where are you going?" he asked.

She composed herself enough to speak. "Eastly," she murmured.

"Eastly isn't far out of my way. Look, I think that may have been the guy who's on the news. Why don't I drive you the rest of the way. We can inform the police there and arrange for your car to be retrieved later."

Again she looked uneasy but nodded in agreement. She sat rigidly in the passenger seat, clutching her bag to her.

"Shall we put that on the floor," he said, "then you can put your seatbelt on." He gently prised the bag from her grasp and put it on the floor in front of her.

Seatbelts fastened Tom started the car and pulled away. He glanced at the girl. Quite pretty, he thought, though he had never really gone for blondes himself. She had a cute little pixy face though which suited the short hair style.

"So, what's your name?" he ventured.

By now she was leaning right up against the passenger door as if to keep as far away from him as possible. "Sara," she answered him.

"Nice name. This guy who tried to attack you, did you get a look at him?"

Sara shook her head. "Not really. It was dark and I just wanted to get away."

At an empty junction ahead the traffic lights turned to red. Tom slowed down and stopped even though there wasn't another vehicle in sight. He turned to look at Sara who was just bending down to get something from her bag.

He froze.

The lights changed to green but the car did not move. They changed to red again and again back to green. Still the car remained stationary. The passenger door opened and the pretty girl with short blonde hair got out and started running down the road.

A passing red Peugeot stopped to pick her up. The driver listened to her story, calmed her down and finally she settled in the front passenger seat. He turned off his radio in order to give her his attention.

Behind them the traffic lights continued to move through their sequence but the driver of the black mini did not respond. The radio inside was still on. A spokesman from the local psychiatric hospital was being interviewed.

"*The patient's name is Sara Wilkins. She is 22 years old, medium height and build and has short, blonde hair. Sara is highly manipulative and is adept at gaining people's confidence. Be in no doubt, however, that she is extremely disturbed and dangerous and should not be approached on any account. We also have reason to believe that she may be armed.*"

Sara put her bag on the floor in front of her and fastened her seatbelt. She turned to the driver and smiled.

First published in The Weekly News, 2010

The Christmas Do

by Rob Nisbet

It's perverse, I know, but the thing I enjoy most about being a temp is also the thing I most dread – starting somewhere new.

The first day is always a nightmare. Of course everyone remembers me, Suzie, the new temp, but I'm always confused by the unfamiliar names and faces. I try to make a good impression but I never know what to wear, can't work the photocopier and I don't know the way to the ladies.

On the plus side, I like to think of first days as a bit of an adventure. What does it matter what I do or say? I've got a built-in safety net. I know that in a few weeks, or months at most, I'm able to leave everything behind and I'll be off doing something else, trying something new.

Rico says I'm just restless and I guess he's right. I couldn't stand doing the same thing day after day. It surprises Rico that we've stayed together for so long, about two years now. That's a record for me; I guess there are some things I don't get bored with.

But, work's different. Whatever tedious task I'm given to do, I know there is always a light at the end of the tunnel. And that suits me. I like my life the way it is: a bit of excitement, dash of the unknown, not yet rutted into a routine.

My first day at Frinton Insurance started reasonably well. It was a chilly winter's day, but I had been shown to a desk in a bright warm open-plan office. The desk came with a name plate:

'Carol Prince'. I slid this to one side. This was *my* desk now; for the next few weeks at least. I adjusted Carol's chair to my height and familiarised myself with my new surroundings and neighbours.

One thing struck me instantly – their clothes.

All the women were what I'd call over-glammed. Not tarty, but not usual office wear either. Their hair was made-up, faces painted, hems a little too high, tops a little too low for the December chill. They made me feel distinctly underdressed in my plain trouser suit and white blouse. Then came the explanation – in the form of Glen.

Glen was ambling in my direction, I could hardly miss him. He was what Rico calls a gym-freak - that's what he calls any man more muscular than himself. Glen was tall and heavy with broad shoulders. His hair was thick and dark, with eyebrows and meticulously-shaped stubble to match. He crossed the room and sat sideways on my desk.

"So," he said, "you're the new Carol." His mouth was a grim line, as if to match his square jaw.

"I'm Suzie," I managed to say, somewhat phased by the trim backside planted directly in front of me.

"Glen," he said, tapping his chest. "Listen – Suzie, was it? I've got a problem." He leant closer.

Well, I had a problem too. With presumptuous men sitting on my desk, too close and looming over me.

"Thing is," Glen continued. "It's the Christmas do tonight." He picked up the nameplate, casually flicking it into the air and catching it again. "I'm the organiser, and now that 'Christmas Carol' can't make it, I'm one girl short. How about it?"

He oozed smarmy confidence.

"That's – really nice of you…" I was annoyed that I sounded so hesitant. I was expecting the usual pile of filing on my desk first thing, not an invitation – and Glen's bum. "But," I continued, "it's my first morning – I don't know anyone."

"Come out tonight then – get to know us."

89

I *was* tempted – it would break the first-day-ice. And Rico wouldn't mind. He works most evenings so it's not like he'd be alone in the flat waiting for me. And I could easily text him; tell him what I was up to.

Glen scratched a hand across his stubbled chin. "Straight after work," he said. "The little Latin bar, near the station."

That clinched it for me – somewhere I knew. "That's a coincidence…" I said, but didn't get any further.

"You know the place?" Glen didn't wait for an answer. He rocked his left hand in front of me, as if he could sway my decision one way or the other. No ring, I noticed. "Bit of exotic grub," he said, "bit of dancing. And you'd be doing me a favour – even out my numbers."

"OK," I said. "I'll come along."

"I knew you would." Glen slid from the desk. "It's fifteen quid for the food – drinks are extra when we get there."

He sauntered back to a group of male colleagues. "Number problem solved," he told them. He jerked a thumb in my direction, not caring that I could still hear him. "New girl's coming." How I longed then for that great pile of filing – anything to distract me from the many sets of eyes that swung in my direction.

A couple of the girls had taken me under their wing, Kate and Pam. The little Latin bar was snug and cosy, and we chose a corner table to be near the band. I'd heard this group play before and knew the evening was in good hands. They beat out a correct four-beat salsa; the sound of rhythmic guitars and measured percussion pulsated over us and I found myself swaying and tapping my feet.

Kate leant across our dimly-lit table, strings of Christmas lights reflecting in our growing collection of empty glasses.

"Glen's been telling anyone who'll listen, that you only came along tonight to do him a favour."

Somehow I wasn't surprised.

"He would say that," chuckled Pam. "Have you noticed yet, Suzie, how the whole world revolves around Glen?"

I laughed. "He does seem to have an inflated opinion of himself."

I glanced towards to the bar with its exotic array of coloured bottles. Glen leant over it, gesturing with his arms, chatting to the girl who was serving. She was smiling, or perhaps she was trying not to laugh at the bright Santa hat he was wearing.

Kate followed my gaze. "He's certainly good looking…" she began, then stopped. I could feel her eyes on me, testing my reaction.

"Yeah," I agreed. "But doesn't he know it!"

It was the correct answer, and our little table dissolved into conspiratorial giggles.

Pam nudged my elbow. "Hey, Suzie. Have you noticed that waiter? He was behind the bar, now he's over there collecting glasses." A sing-song lilt seeped into her voice, *"He keeps looking at you."*

I gave him a quick glance. Yes, of course I had noticed him. At that instant our eyes met, and held, just for a moment. Dark eyes, almost black in the subdued light. His head bobbed slightly to the rhythmic music, he winked and flashed the briefest of smiles.

I didn't think anyone else had noticed, but Pam nudged me again. "Hey, Suzie. Looks like Christmas has come early."

That was when Glen interrupted. He loomed over our table in his flamboyant red hat, his grim mouth twisted into a leering grin. "You ladies not dancing?" he said, then held his hand out to Pam. She rolled her eyes, but took his hand anyway. As they crossed to the small dance area, Glen leant back and pointed straight at me. "You're next," he announced, as if bestowing some honour.

Glen led Pam to the centre of the floor, and, sure of his audience, called out to the nearest waiter – *my waiter*. "Hey, you! Another round, over here – pronto."

The band was great, but, try as they might, they couldn't get their guitars and percussion to match Glen's gyrations. Not that it bothered him. Glen strutted through a series of disco moves like the lead in some eighties dance movie. He twirled Pam with one arm, swung his hips from side to side and began a frantic stamping that jarred with the four-beat rhythm.

Yes, to the uninformed masses, Glen did look impressive. Self-confidence, apparently, could over-ride any lack of expertise. But his writhing lunges were wildly out of step with the pulse of the music. He had no rhythm and he certainly couldn't salsa.

Glen swung Pam around and ended with a flourish of stamping, arms upraised as in a Spanish flamenco. The man had no idea!

The music stopped and Pam headed quickly back towards our table. She looked relieved that her dance was over. Then with horror I realized that I was next.

The band had formed themselves into a small huddle and I realized that the man I thought of as 'my waiter' was speaking to them. Perhaps they'd be kind to me; perhaps there was some hope after all.

Glen pulled me to my feet, as the maracas and guitars started again – and I realised with relief that it was a sequence I recognised.

Glen however, seemed to regard the music as some irrelevant accompaniment to his hideous lunging. He shook his hips, legs flicking one way then another. I didn't know which way he was going to lunge next and ended-up trotting behind him, trying to fit in, knowing that I must look ridiculous. This was not the good first impression I had hoped for. Then Glen lifted one of my arms, holding my hand high, and I realised that he expected me to twirl myself underneath it.

I could see my waiter, watching, beyond Glen, at the edge of the dance area – so I went for it. I twirled as Glen expected me to, but I didn't stop. I twirled straight into the arms of the waiter. The band stepped up the tempo and my waiter went straight into a step-slide-step-clap, I joined-in gratefully. We moved in instant union, side-stepping a bemused Glen with a step-turn-step-clap.

Kate and Pam gaped at us in a mixture of astonishment and obvious delight, then they joined in the clapping. We must have looked impressive; we were soon surrounded by a ring of spectators swaying and clapping to the beat of the dance. Glen watched too, side-lined, ignored, still wearing his silly Santa hat.

My waiter and I turned to face each other, he grinned broadly and I couldn't help doing the same as we slipped almost naturally into a series of complementary moves.

And did I feel any pang of guilt about Glen? No, not a jot. And anyway, I was only the temp, what had he called me, new-girl? So what if he hated me after this, that was another joy of being able to move on in a few weeks.

From then on it was a brilliant night. My waiter and I were persuaded to perform a few exhibition pieces, fitting them around his other duties. And now that Glen's uncoordinated stumbling had been exposed, it was surprising how many people were happy to speak out about his general insolence and selfish attitude.

Glen spent the rest of the evening propping up the bar. He'd removed the hat – clearly he no longer wanted to be the centre of attention.

I confessed then, to Kate and Pam, that I'd attended salsa classes for the past two years, with my boyfriend, Rico. I knew from experience that I'd be labelled now as, Suzie – the one who could dance.

That's another quirk of temping. As soon as people find out something about you, they latch onto it and think they know your whole life story. So at Frinton Insurance I'll be remembered as, Suzie – wasn't she the one who could salsa? Or perhaps – wasn't she the girl who pricked Glen's ego? Seems my first day wasn't so bad after all.

Perhaps, before I move on to my next job, I'll let Kate and Pam into my other little secret. That Rico and I had been rehearsing those steps for weeks at our salsa class, and that Rico works most evenings – in a certain little Latin bar near the station.

Twenty-One Today

by Linda Barrett

Ciara woke with a start. She reached out a trembling hand and switched on the bedside lamp. The alarm clock read 3am. She was sweating but felt chilled to the bone. She put on her dressing gown and went downstairs to make herself a hot drink.

The kettle was just coming to the boil as her mother came into the kitchen.

"Nightmares again?" she looked concerned.

Ciara nodded. "You'd think I'd be used to them by now, wouldn't you?"

"Ciara, your 21st birthday is only two days away. Once it's over I'm sure the dreams will stop."

"Yes, one way or another they will," she poured out their teas.

"Don't say that."

The dreams had started on Ciara's seventh birthday. It'd been her first birthday, in this house, with these wonderful people who she thought of as her parents. Ciara had always known that she was adopted. Her exotic looks aside; it had never been kept from her. She thought she could vaguely remember being brought here when she was six years old. Before that she had no clear memories at all.

Her seventh birthday had been a wonderful day with a big party and lots of presents. She'd been exhausted when she'd finally fallen into bed but her sleep had been fitful. She'd woken up in the early hours of the morning, screaming.

This was to be a nightmare that would haunt her all of her life. Sometimes in her waking hours as well as in her sleep.

Jess Harding sat at the table, across from her daughter, and looked into her anxious face. She reached out and put a comforting hand on her arm. "We are going to celebrate this birthday," she said with conviction. "And I've got a feeling we'll be celebrating your engagement to Joe soon, too. You'll see."

Ciara nodded but said nothing.

The big day dawned warm and sunny. In contrast Ciara woke up shivering, her stomach in knots. She got up, showered and went downstairs.

"I thought you'd just like some cereal as we're going out to lunch," Jess held out the box to her as she entered the kitchen. "No thanks Mum, coffee will be fine." She started to open the cards which had been placed in a neat pile in the middle of the table. Then she started on her presents.

"We saved this one till last," her father beamed as he held out a large box. She managed a smile and opened it up. It was a DVD player.

"Thanks Dad. It's brilliant."

"I'll go up and install it in your bedroom," he said.

"How are you feeling?" asked Jess once he'd gone.

"Scared," was all she said.

The older woman looked at her daughter's anxious face.

"Don't let it spoil your day, love. We'll laugh about this tomorrow. You'll see."

Ciara tried very hard not to let it spoil her day. Her parents and Joe took her to an upmarket restaurant, in the city, for lunch. She tried for their sake but the food turned to sawdust in her mouth. Lunch was followed by a matinee performance at the theatre. It was a comedy but try as she might Ciara found it impossible to concentrate. The day ended at home where all her friends had gathered for a surprise party. They'd even got the food ready and decorated the house while Ciara was out. It was wonderful and by the end of it she started to relax. Joe was the last to leave.

He held Ciara close. "Will you marry me?" he whispered as he was about to go.

"Ask me again tomorrow Joe. I'll give you an answer then. And I'll explain why I've been so on edge of late."

"I'll be round early," he said, and he left.

True to his word Joe arrived at the house just after nine. Jess met him at the door. She looked strained, he thought.

"Are you okay?" he asked.

"Yes, of course I am, Joe. I'll just go up and see if Ciara's awake yet." As she spoke they heard a noise coming from upstairs. Jess' face noticeably relaxed. "Oh, no need. That sounds like her."

A few moments later Ciara came running downstairs and into the kitchen. She hugged them both. Joe thought he saw tears in Jess's eyes as she stood up.

"Get yourself a coffee, love. Your dad's in the shed. I'll go and see if he needs a hand."

"What on earth's going on?" Joe asked once they were alone.

She sat down at the table opposite him and took both his hands in hers.

"You're going to think I'm totally crazy but here goes." She took a deep breath. "Since I was about seven I've had this recurring nightmare. I saw my own death. Well not saw it exactly but felt it. It was a shocking, violent death. All the dreams were the same and whatever it was that happened always happened on my 21st birthday. I saw the cake clearly. It had pink and white icing with a pink candle in the middle and the words '*Happy 21st Ciara!*' iced onto it. It's driven me crazy all these years. In the end I honestly believed that yesterday would be my last day on Earth."

Joe squeezed her hands. "Why on earth didn't you tell me?"

"I don't know. It all seemed so real and yet so stupid at the same time. Mum and Dad were the only people in the world who knew. Dad never really took it seriously. He thought it was just a dream. I think it's always worried Mum though."

"Hey, the day has passed now and you're still here so," he moved around to her side of the table and got down on one knee. He took her hand in his, "Will you marry me?"

Ciara's face lit up. "Yes," she said.

He kissed her. "I've got an idea. Why don't we get married a year from now? We'll do it on your 22nd birthday. It'll make it doubly special."

Everyone thought this was a brilliant idea and for once Ciara and her parents spent a happy and stress-free year. They relished in all the plans and preparations and finally the big day arrived.

It was perfect and at the evening reception there was a surprise visitor. Fiona Jenkins arrived unannounced. Fiona had handled Ciara's adoption all those years ago. Ciara didn't remember her but her parents were both surprised and pleased to see her.

The bride and groom were ready to leave. "I'll just get my bag from the front porch," said Ciara. "It was very nice to meet you Fiona."

"Likewise," said Fiona. "I do hope you don't mind me barging in," she said to Jess after Ciara had gone, "But this was the first adoption I'd organised. And this is such a momentous occasion being her 21st birthday as well."

"No, you've got that wrong Fiona. Today is her 22nd birthday."

"Ah, you forget dear, she was born in Korea. By their reckoning she is twenty-two. That's because in Korea children are deemed to be one year old at birth. But by our reckoning this is her twenty-first birthday as well as her wedding day. I thought that might be overlooked so I brought a little something to mark it."

She handed Jess a box.

It was at that moment that they heard the deafening crash. The house shuddered violently.

The police said later that the truck driver had probably fallen asleep at the wheel. He veered off the road and straight into the front porch of the house. It was terribly tragic but also lucky that Ciara had been the only one in there at the time. The death toll could have been much higher, they'd said.

That evening Jess was being cared for in her neighbour's living room. She suddenly noticed the box that Fiona had given to her earlier lying on the floor. Someone must have brought it in here she thought. She took off the lid and froze in horror. Inside was an exquisite pink and white birthday cake. It had a pink candle in the middle and the words '*Happy 21st Ciara!*' iced on the top.

First published in That's Life Fast Fiction, 2009

TURN AROUND

by Rob Nisbet

Anyway, I said to Bernice, just last week, "Bernice," I said, "forget him. He's just a man. He's not worth all the hassle. Men," I said, "are only good for *one* thing, if you know what I mean, *two*, at a pinch, if you include *hanging wallpaper*." That made Bernice smile, that did, which was a good sign, you see, I think she'd already decided by then to leave him.

But, *you know Bernice*. She's a worrier, she had to be sure, *really sure*, that breaking up with Simon was what she wanted.

So I asked Bernice what the problem *was*. "Bernice," I said, "what's the problem?" and you know what she said? She said that it was *her*. Her! Simon, it seemed had lost interest and was taking her for granted – and *she*, poor girl, was blaming herself.

Anyway, I told her, "Bernice," I said, "you're too good for him. If a man loses interest in his partner, it's simply because he's a man – they don't know any better, poor sods. They get too comfortable – start collecting beer mats or filthy magazines. If Simon's treating you like just another beer mat," I said, "then dump him."

But Bernice still wanted to be sure. She thought, you see, that she still loved him. And she *hoped* Simon still loved her. Physically things were okay – there was no problem with – you know – '*hanging wallpaper*', but that's not love is it? - not really.

So what's a girl to do? Feeling insecure and stuck with a dud fella? "Bernice," I told her, "I have the solution; I'm taking you shopping! What you need is a confidence boost. A really great dress, designer handbag, we'll re-style your hair and have a facial." I knew of this great place in town, *not cheap*, but cheap's not what Bernice needed; you know, you can't restore a girl's ego on a shoestring. And you should have *seen* the difference. I could hardly get her away from the mirrors, she was so pleased, and it's strange, she related everything back to Simon. What her *perfect* Simon would think, what her *perfect* Simon would say, how much *perfect* Simon would love her in her new outfit. How *obsessive* is that? Anyway, Bernice came out simply glowing with confidence – a new woman. I said to her, "Bernice," I said, "you're a new woman. Now, go and stun that man of yours; he won't know what's hit him."

Anyway, that evening – it was Simon's turn to cook, so he'd ordered a takeaway and was having a beer when Bernice walked in.

She gave him five minutes. Five *whole* minutes, to say something, or at least to notice. Five minutes is a long time when your world is crumbling dry-as-dust around you, when every inconsequential remark Simon made showed Bernice how shallow and self-centred he really was.

Then, you know what she did? She tipped the beer over his head and stormed out. And he was calling after her, "What have I done? What have I done?" He'd got no idea – *typical*.

Anyway, Bernice stayed with me that night – what are friends for? I told her, "Bernice," I said, "I've got a spare room, and there's no man around to cause you any grief; you can stay as long as you like." But it was just the one night, the very next day she'd organised renting a place of her own. You see, she can be quite determined, Bernice, when she wants to be.

That was last week, then, on Saturday I helped her to move some of her things out of Simon's place. She didn't want to meet him, you see, so I said I'd go.

Simon was there, ready with the boxes. He seemed quite bewildered – in that pathetic *lost* way men have.

Anyway, Bernice was still seething. I said to her, "Bernice," I said, "now's your chance to move on…" And she agreed. She said that from now on she was going to be more like *me* – single, no ties, no irritating compromises, she'd be able to do *whatever* she wanted, *whenever* she wanted. She said that she'd been given her freedom, been given back her life.

I said to her, "Good for you, Bernice," I said. And I meant it too. She's far happier now, quite turned her life around. What a difference a week makes.

I'm not sure though about her modelling her life on mine. It's true, you know, that I'm not attached, *not at the moment*, but I don't intend to stay that way forever. In fact, you know, now that I've met her *perfect* Simon, I'm thinking of having a *turn around* in my life as well.

Updating Dora

by Linda Barrett

Dora sighed as the rock song on Clare's mobile sounded out yet again.

"You're very welcome to give your friends my phone number, you know, if you want them to ring while you're here."

"No, it's alright, Gran, everyone's got my mobile number. You should get one. A lot of people your age have them these days."

Dora sniffed. "I don't think so, one phone is quite enough, thank you."

Clare looked heavenwards. "Honestly Gran, you're so techno phobic."

"Well, when would I use it? I don't need a mobile phone."

"Okay, you might be out shopping and need to ring someone. There aren't as many phone boxes around as there used to be. You're always complaining about them being vandalised. I don't know why you trek around town and the supermarket anyway. Lots of people get their shopping online these days."

"But I don't possess a computer, nor do I wish to. Secondly, I've been doing my shopping this way for the best part of sixty years and I'll carry on if it's all the same to you. Online! Indeed!"

●●●

It was raining hard when Dora, laden with shopping bags, saw her bus pull in at the bus stop. Damn! If she missed it she'd have to wait another half an hour and she'd be drenched. She started to hurry along the pavement, her eyes locked on her goal. She was about a hundred yards away when she tripped. The next thing she knew she was sprawled on the pavement. She looked up to see the bus pull away and her heart sank. People started to gather around.

"Are you alright?" a kindly lady asked as she bent over her.

Dora didn't know if she was or not. She could feel a searing pain in her ankle. A young man offered to help her up but, even with his assistance she couldn't put her weight on it. The young man took out a mobile phone from his jeans pocket and called an ambulance.

●●●

"You haven't done much damage," a young doctor informed her. Dora wondered how long ago he had left school.

"You've sprained your ankle quite badly but aside from a few bruises that seems to be it. I think we'll keep you in overnight though just to be on the safe side."

The next morning Clare went to the hospital.

"Mum's coming later to take you to our house Gran. She says you can't go home on your own, you wouldn't manage."

"Nonsense, I'm perfectly alright."

Just the same Dora's youngest daughter, Sue, arrived late that afternoon and after some consultation with the doctor insisted on taking her home.

●●●

To Dora's surprise she actually spent three very enjoyable days with Sue and Clare. On her first night there her son, Jack phoned from Australia to make sure she was alright. Dora was touched but afterwards chided Sue for telling him.

"There's no need for such a fuss," she said, as she carefully lowered herself back onto the sofa. "I've only had a bit of a fall."

Sue grunted. "Did you speak to the children?"

"Yes, I had a little chat with both of them." She loved speaking to the children but always felt a little sad afterwards. She missed them so much and wasn't able to speak to them as often as she would like.

By the end of the third day Dora was becoming restless and wanted to get home and back to her own bed.

Sue eventually relented and drove her there. Clare went with them for the ride.

"Now, you're sure you'll be alright Mum?"

"I can stay for a few days if you want, Gran"

"Don't be so silly; get off the pair of you."

Reluctantly they left.

About six weeks after Dora's accident. She and her granddaughter were sitting at the kitchen table with their hands wrapped around mugs of hot chocolate. Suddenly the door bell rang. Oh, that'll be my shopping," said Dora getting up.

"What?"

"Close your mouth, dear. It's most unladylike.

The next thing a burly young man was carrying bags of shopping in. Clare gasped.

"Right, you can help me put this lot away," she smiled at her after he'd gone.

"I decided you were right," she said as they worked. "Oh, don't get me wrong, I still think there's a lot to be said for going out shopping. You get fresh air and exercise, not to mention the contact. On the other hand there's not much to be said for having to go out in all weathers and carrying back heavy bags. Sometimes it's nice to have someone deliver it."

"But how did you order it?"

Dora went into the living room and to Clare's further astonishment she came back carrying a laptop. She put it on the kitchen table and opened it.

"I'll just boot it up, shall I?" she said as she sat down and hit the power button.

"This is the latest technology, Gran! When did you get it?"

"I got it soon after the accident. The man at the shop said I should get the latest technology because it's easier to use. Bob next door came in every evening for two weeks to show me what to do. He got me online and then I did a free Internet course at the library. They taught me all about e-mails and surfing. Oh look, your Uncle Jack's online. He's an early bird. It must only be about 7am over there. Do you want to chat to him?"

They spent a pleasant hour chatting to Jack and his family. Finally, it was time for Clare to go.

"I'm really pleased you decided to move into the 21st century," she said to Dora as she was putting on her coat.

"Are you coming next week?"

"Of course! Why?"

Dora opened a drawer in the hall table and took out a box. She handed it to her.

"Gran! You've got a mobile phone!"

"Well, I thought that at least if I do have an accident when I'm out I can ring for help myself. Will you show me how it works next week?"

"Course I will. You have to be the coolest gran in the world," she said and she gave Dora an extra big hug.

After Clare had left Dora went back upstairs. She sat down and went back online. 'Bargain flights to Australia' she typed and clicked 'search'. Well, it was time she met the grandchildren. They wrote such lovely e-mails!

First published in the '100 Stories for Haiti' charity anthology, 2010

Printed in Great Britain
by Amazon